HIS LITTLE GIRL

Staying alone at her brother-in-law's cottage on a stormy night, Dora finds an intruder in the house, a man called John Gannon. He's clearly a man on the run, but Dora is charmed by him — and the adorable little girl in his arms. She decides to help Gannon, a devoted father, willing to do anything to keep Sophie safe. Too bad the only thing keeping Dora safe from Gannon is his misconception that she is Richard's wife . . .

LIZ FIELDING

HIS LITTLE GIRL

Complete and Unabridged

LINFORD
Leicester

First published in Great Britain in 1998

First Linford Edition
published 2009

British Library CIP Data

Fielding, Liz
   His little girl.—Large print ed.—
Linford romance library
   1. Love stories
   2. Large type books
   I. Title
   823.9'2 [F]

   ISBN 978–1–84782–527–8

Published by
F. A. Thorpe (Publishing)
Anstey, Leicestershire

Set by Words & Graphics Ltd.
Anstey, Leicestershire
Printed and bound in Great Britain by
T. J. International Ltd., Padstow, Cornwall

This book is printed on acid-free paper

1

Something woke Dora. One minute she was sleeping, the next wide awake, her ears straining through all the familiar night noises of the countryside for the out-of-place sound that had woken her.

She had fled to the country for peace, but after the constant traffic noise of London she'd found the quiet almost eerie the first night she'd stayed alone at Richard and Poppy's cottage. Soon, though, her ears had adjusted to the different sounds of the countryside, and she'd realised that what had at first seemed like silence was subverted by all manner of small noises.

Now she lay quite still, listening to the familiar night time orchestra. The gentle gurgling of the small river less than a hundred yards from the door of the cottage as it swirled through the reeds; the slow trickle of rain along the guttering; the sombre dripping as the trees shed the water dumped by a passing scurry of rain.

Punctuating these watery sounds there was the irritable grumbling of a duck, itself disturbed by something. A fox, perhaps? The first time Dora had heard the unearthly rattle made by the night-time hunter her blood had run quite cold; after a week at the cottage she was not so timid.

She swung out of bed and crossed swiftly to the window, ready to fling abuse, and whatever else came to hand, at the marauding intruder. But the landscape, momentarily bleached by a high, white moon as the scudding rainclouds cleared, revealed the dark humps of sleeping ducks. On the surface the riverbank seemed peaceful enough. Not a fox, then.

She propped her elbows on the window ledge for a moment, resting her chin on her hands, and leaned forward to breathe in the night air. It was full of the rich, mingled scents of honeysuckle, stocks and the roses climbing against the wall beneath her window, under-scored, after the sudden shower of rain, by the heavy sweetness of damp earth. It was such an English smell, she thought, something to be treasured after the stomach-churning horrors she had encountered in the refugee camps.

Then, in the far distance, there was a glimmer of lightning followed by a low rumble of thunder moving away with the rainclouds. Dora gave a little shiver and pulled the window shut. It was undoubtedly the thunder that had woken her, and, trapped in the Thames Valley, it would be back. The thought raised gooseflesh that shivered over her skin.

She rubbed her arms and turned quickly from the window to reach for her silk wrap, knowing that with thunder on the loose she wouldn't be able to go back to sleep. Downstairs she could switch on the hi-fi to drown out the noise, and she could always catch up on sleep later — one of the many pleasures of being entirely on her own, with a telephone number that no one but close family knew.

She raised the latch on the bedroom door, stepped onto the landing. She'd make some tea first and then . . .

And then she heard the sound again, and knew that it hadn't been thunder that had woken her.

It had sounded almost like a cough, a harsh, crackling little cough — the kind a sick child would make and it had been so close that it could have been inside the cottage.

But that was ridiculous. The cottage had a comprehensive security system. Her brother-in-law had fitted it after a vagrant had got in and made himself at home. It wouldn't happen again, and any casual burglar would be put off too. And she was sure she hadn't left a window open.

Almost sure.

She leaned forward over the stairs, listening for what seemed an age. But there was nothing, only a quiet so intense that the nervous thudding of her heart began to pound in her ears.

Had she imagined the sound? She took one step down. The cottage was miles from the nearest road, for heaven's sake, it had been raining on and off all evening and no one in their right mind would have a child out so late, certainly not a sick one. She glanced at her watch, it was too dark to see but it had to be long past midnight.

She took another step. She'd noticed how oddly sound carried across the river. Perhaps, after all, it had been the cry of some small animal, the sound magnified in the deep silence of the night. Yet still she hesitated on the stairs.

Then a rumble of thunder, low and threatening, almost overhead as the storm bounced off the hills and swung back down the valley, drove everything else from her head and sent her racing down the stairs to seek the sanctuary of the living room. But even as she reached for the light switch she knew that thunder was the least of her problems, and her hand instead flew to her mouth as, momentarily illuminated by the moonlight streaming in through the windows, she saw a child, a little girl, her thin face gaunt with tiredness.

She was standing in the middle of the living room, and for one ghastly moment Dora was quite certain that she had seen a ghost. Then the child coughed again. Dora was no expert on the subject, but she was pretty sure that ghosts didn't cough.

Yet, shivering beneath the thin blanket that she clutched about her, dark untidy hair clinging damply to her sallow skin, tiny feet quite bare, the child was quite the most miserable looking little creature that she had ever seen outside a refugee camp.

For a moment she was riveted to the spot, uncertain what to do — not scared, exactly, but unnerved by the sudden appearance of this strange child in the middle of her sister's living room, her eyes enormous in her thin little face as she stared at Dora. There was something unsettling about the child's wary stillness.

Then, as common sense reasserted itself, she told herself there was nothing to fear. No matter where the child had come from, she was in need of warmth and comfort, and she surged across the carpet, her own bare feet making no sound as she swept the child into her arms, holding her close to warm her with her own body.

For a moment the little girl's eyes widened with silent fear, and she remained rigid against her, but Dora made soothing little noises, as she would have done to any small, frightened creature.

'It's all right, sweetheart,' she murmured, her voice barely above a whisper. 'There's nothing to be afraid of.' The child stared at her, flinching momentarily as Dora's hand stroked her forehead, pushing back the damp tendrils of hair. Her skin was hot and dry, her complexion unhealthily flushed despite her sallow skin.

Whoever she was, one thing was certain: she should be in bed, not wandering about on a stormy night, straying into strange houses. And she needed a doctor.

'What's your name, kitten?' she murmured, leaving the other questions that were crowding in on her to be answered in their own good time. Not least, how she had managed to get into the cottage.

The little girl stared at Dora for a moment, and then, with something between a sigh and a moan, she let her head fall against Dora's shoulder. She weighed nothing, and most of that was blanket. Dora pushed the horrible thing away and enveloped the child in her silk wrap. Who was she? Where on earth — ?

The question remained unasked as there was a sudden crash from beyond the living room door, a low curse in a man's voice.

The child, it seemed, was not alone.

And Dora, suddenly quite shockingly angry, decided that she wanted a few words with whatever kind of burglar dragged a sick child about with him on his nocturnal activities. Without considering the possibility that her second uninvited guest might, unlike the child, present a very real source of danger, she flung open the door and snapped on the light.

'What the — ?' The intruder, swinging round from a cupboard, a torch in his hand, blinked blindly in the sudden light, throwing up the hand holding the torch to shade his eyes. Then he saw Dora. 'Good God!' he exclaimed. 'Who the devil are you?'

Dora snapped. Ignoring the fact that he was the better part of a head taller than her, and could have picked her up as easily as she had lifted the infant in her arms, ignoring the fact that he looked as if he had been sleeping beneath a hedge for a week, she came right back at him.

'Who the devil wants to know?'

The man stiffened at this attack. 'I do.' Then, quite unexpectedly, he dropped the arm shading his face and smiled. Dora's sister was a model, Dora had seen professionals smile. This man was good. And he moved towards her, totally at ease with the situation. 'I'm sorry. I didn't mean to shout, but you startled me — '

'I startled *you*?' Dora gaped at him, momentarily stunned by his nerve. Then she gathered herself. 'How did you get in here?' she demanded.

'I picked the lock,' he said, with disarming candour. He was regarding her with open curiosity, not in the least embarrassed by such a confession. 'I thought the cottage was empty.'

Picked the lock? He admitted it, and smiled as he said it, without an ounce of shame or remorse. Challenged like this, any ordinary burglar would have done the decent thing and taken to his heels. She hefted the child in her arms, fitting her more comfortably to her hip. But then ordinary burglars didn't take sick children with them when they went about their nightly forays.

'Well, as you can see, it's not empty. I live here, mister,' she declared, ignoring her own temporary status during her sister's absence as a mere detail. When Poppy had offered her the use of the cottage while she and Richard were away she had been instructed to treat the place as if it were her own, but with privileges came responsibility. Right now, Dora decided it was time to take her responsibilities seriously. So she glared at the intruder, refusing to be charmed by an overgrown tramp with a practised smile, who was obviously looking for somewhere dry to bed down for the night. 'I live here,' she repeated, 'and I don't take in lodgers, paying or otherwise, so you'd better get moving.'

The smile abruptly vanished. 'I'll move when I'm good and ready — ' he began.

'Tell that to the police; they'll be here any minute — ' As her voice rose the child in her arms began to wail, a thin, painful little cry that distracted Dora so that she turned to the child, hushing her gently as she stroked her hair. 'What on earth are you doing out with a sick child at this time of night anyway?' she demanded, as the little girl quietened under her touch. 'She should be in bed.'

'That's exactly where I was planning to put her, just as soon as I'd warmed her some milk,' he said tightly, confirming her suspicions. He made a slight gesture at a carton of milk on the table, as if it provided him with some sort of alibi. 'I didn't expect to find anyone here.'

'So you said.' Dora ignored the fact that his voice belied his torn, muddy jeans, a grubby sweater and a soft leather bomber jacket that had once cost a fortune but had seen some very hard wear since, and was now coming unstitched at the seams. A tramp with a public school accent was still a tramp. 'I suppose you were planning to squat?'

'Of course not.' A fleeting glance of

irritation crossed the man's face and he shrugged. 'Richard won't mind me staying for a few days.'

'Richard!' Her eyebrows rose as he made free with her brother-in-law's name.

'Richard Marriott,' he elaborated. 'The owner of this cottage.'

'I know who Richard Marriott is. And you'll pardon me if I differ with you regarding his reaction. I happen to know that he takes a very dim view of breaking and entering.'

This declaration seemed to amuse her intruder. 'Unless he's the one doing it. I should know — he's the one who taught me enough to get in here.' He looked her in the eye and defied her to tell him otherwise.

'Richard uses his skills to test security systems,' she protested. 'Not for house-breaking.'

'That's true,' he conceded.

Gannon regarded the young woman who was defying him with concern. She was either crazy, or a whole lot tougher than she looked, standing there in nothing but a satin nightdress which clung to her in a manner that would give a monk ideas. The wrap that might have given her some measure of decency had been untied and thrown about Sophie, to warm her. Well, even the toughest women have their weaknesses, he thought, weaknesses that just this once he would be forced to turn to his own advantage.

He took a step forward. She didn't retreat, but stood her ground and stared him down. 'I'll take Sophie,' he said, and saw the flash of concern that lit something deep in dark grey eyes that a moment before had been simply hostile. He struggled with guilt at what he was about to do. But Sophie was at the end of her tether, and he would do whatever it took to make his daughter safe.

'Take her?'

'You asked us to leave.' He reached for the child. Sophie grumbled sleepily as he disturbed her, and the woman stepped back, holding the child protectively to her chest.

'Where? Where will you go?' she demanded.

He shrugged. 'Maybe I'll find a barn. Come on, sweetheart, we've disturbed this lady long enough.'

'No — ' He managed to look puzzled. 'You can't take her back out there. She's got a temperature.'

Bingo. 'Has she?' He put his hand on Sophie's head and gave a resigned shrug. 'Maybe you're right. It's been a tough few days.' He put his hands lightly beneath the child's arms, as if planning to take her. 'But don't worry. We'll manage . . . somehow.'

She was torn. He saw the momentary struggle darken her eyes. She wanted him to go, but her conscience wouldn't allow her to send Sophie out into the night. 'You might. She won't,' she said, as her conscience won. 'I thought you were going to warm her some milk?'

He glanced at the carton of milk standing on the cupboard, alongside a

Sussex trug overflowing with an artfully casual arrangement of dried flowers. Beside it a couple of shabby waxed jackets hung from a Shaker peg rail. Very classy. The last time he had been at the cottage this had been little more than a scullery. Now it was an entrance lobby straight out of *Homes and Gardens*, quarry-tiled and expensively rustic.

He turned back to the young woman who, if he was clever enough, would any minute be urging him to stay. For the sake of the child. It was time to remind her that Richard was his friend. He replaced the torch on the hook behind the door, where he had found it — that at least had not changed since their fishing trips — and picked up the milk.

'Yes, I was.' He indicated the open cupboard in which rubber boots and outdoor shoes were stored instead of the pans he had been expecting. 'In fact I was looking for a saucepan when I disturbed you. What happened to the kitchen? And when did Richard have electricity installed?'

'That's really none of your business,' Dora replied curtly. But it did explain why he had been poking about the cupboards in the dark. It simply hadn't occurred to him to look for a light switch. He might have been to the cottage before, but not in the last twelve months.

Not that she had been impressed with his claim that he knew Richard. Anybody around here would have known that this cottage belonged to Richard Marriott. And if he did know him, so what? He'd still broken in. 'I didn't catch your name,' she said.

'Gannon. John Gannon,' he said, extending his hand formally, as if this was some cocktail party rather than a middle-of-the-night confrontation that should have him cringing with embarrassment.

She could see that he just wasn't the cringing type. On the contrary, his gaze was wandering appreciatively from her tousled hair, over the loose silk wrap, lingering on pink-painted toenails peeping out from beneath the hem of her nightgown, before returning to her face. Then his face creased in a thoughtful frown. 'Have we met somewhere before?'

There had been a lot of publicity when she'd returned from the Balkans; total strangers accosting her in the street, wanting to talk to her, newspapers wanting to write about the 'Sloane' who had given up the social whirl to drive aid trucks across Europe. If he remembered that he would be sure that he had fallen on his feet, sure that she was a soft touch.

It had been the need to get away from all that which had driven Dora down to the cottage in the first place, so, what with one thing and another, it seemed wiser not to jog his memory about where he might have seen her face before. And she ignored his hand, along with his invitation to introduce herself.

She wasn't about to exchange civilities with a common criminal, particularly not one who had broken into her sister's home. Even if he did have a velvet-soft voice, toffee-brown eyes and a deliciously cleft chin. After all the chin hadn't been shaved in several days. And the toffee eyes were taking rather too much liberty with her under-dressed figure for her liking. With the child in her arms, she was unable to do anything about the wrap, but conscious that his gaze had become riveted to her pink toenails, she shuffled them out of sight.

'That's hardly an original pick-up line,' she replied, with a crispness she was far from feeling.

'No,' he agreed, barely able to conceal his amusement, despite his exhaustion. This was one spirited lady. 'I really must try harder.'

'Don't bother.'

'Breaking and entering isn't my usual line of business,' he said, letting his hand fall to his side. He was still regarding her thoughtfully. 'Who *are* you?'

Dora firmly resisted the temptation

to ask him what his 'usual line' was. 'Does it matter who I am?' she asked.

He shrugged. 'I don't suppose it does. But allow me to say that you're a considerable improvement on Elizabeth. She would never have wasted time on anything quite so frivolous as painting her toenails.'

The man was outrageous. Not content with breaking into the cottage, he was flirting with her. Yet, despite her better judgement she was beginning to accept his familiarity with her brother-in-law's personal life.

'Elizabeth?' she probed.

'Elizabeth Marriott. Richard's wife,' he obliged. 'A girl of very little imagination — a lack which was more than made up for by her greed, if the fact that she left him for a banker is anything to judge her by.'

'A banker?' He knew that he was being tested, Dora realised, but that didn't stop her.

'The kind that owns the bank,' he obliged. 'Not the kind who works behind the counter.' And, having apparently awarded himself a pass grade, he made a broad gesture with the milk. 'I never thought he'd sell this place, though.'

'What makes you think he has?'

He looked about him. 'This kind of thing isn't his style.'

It was Dora's turn to smile. 'Maybe you don't know him as well as you think you do.'

He gave her another thoughtful look, then shrugged. 'Shall I heat the milk? Or will you, since everything's been moved?' Not that he had any intention of relieving the woman of her burden. While she was holding Sophie, she was vulnerable to persuasion.

'The kitchen is through there,' she said.

Gannon looked around. More warm earthy colours and glowing wood. 'You've extended into the barn,' he said, reaching for a copper pan and setting it on the hob. 'Is it all like this now?'

'Like what?'

'Like something out of a lifestyle magazine.'

'I don't read lifestyle magazines, so I really couldn't say.' Dora certainly had no intention of getting into a cosy chat about interior decoration with a *common* burglar. No, she corrected herself, the man was far too at ease with himself and his surroundings to be described as a common burglar. She glared at him, but he wasn't in the least bit put out. If anything, she was the one hard pressed to keep up the challenge so she shifted her gaze, glancing down at the child. 'Did you say her name was Sophie?' she enquired. 'Is she your daughter?'

'Yes.' He turned away from her to open the milk and pour some into the pan. 'And yes,' he said.

'Did you know she has a temperature?' Dora pressed.

'You mentioned it.'

'She should see a doctor.'

'I've got some antibiotics for her. All

she needs now is good food and plenty of rest.'

'And this is your idea of giving them to her? The child should be at home with her mother, not being carted about in the middle of the night by an itinerant — '

'Is that what you think?' he interrupted, before she could suggest what kind of itinerant he was, his sideways glance suggesting that she didn't know what she was talking about.

Well, maybe she didn't. But she knew enough to know that Sophie should be at home in bed. Her gaze was drawn back to the exhausted child. Her almost transparent lids were drooping over her eyes. She'd be asleep in a moment. It would be so easy to simply carry her upstairs and pop her into her own warm bed.

'How do you know Richard?' she asked, resisting the temptation to do just that with considerable difficulty.

'We went to the same school.'

'Really?'

'Really.'

Dora wasn't sure what she had expected. Perhaps that they had met through her brother-in-law's burgeoning security business, although whether they had been on the same side was a moot point. But school? While she'd recognised his public school accent, it hadn't occurred to her that he might have shared the same Alma Mater as a future king. A little confused, she said, 'Surely he's older than you?'

'Eight years or thereabouts. He was head boy when I was a very small, very miserable first-year. He rescued me from a bunch of second-year lads who were baiting me because they'd discovered that my mother was unmarried. I don't suppose it happens so much these days. Marriage seems to be a dirty word now.'

'Not to me.' It was difficult to imagine this man ever having being small and vulnerable. 'Richard took you under his wing?'

'It's in his nature to protect the

vulnerable.' He turned back to face her, deeply thoughtful. 'Richard is a *lot* older than you,' he said. 'What's he doing for you?'

'Me?'

'I can't see him going to all this trouble,' he said, glancing around at the expensive rebuilding work, 'just to let the place out. So, has he taken you under his kindly wing, too — or just his brand new duckdown duvet?'

She was about to explain, somewhat indignantly, that Richard was now married to her sister, her seven-years-older sister, when she was interrupted by a sharp rap on the back door.

2

Gannon stiffened, staring towards the back door before turning a fierce, questioning look on her. 'It must be the police,' she muttered, surprising herself with a distinct feeling of discomfort at the thought of handing Gannon over to them.

'The police?'

'I did warn you.' She had, but he clearly hadn't taken her seriously. Then she caught herself. He'd broken in, for heaven's sake. He deserved to be locked up.

'There was no alarm,' he objected.

'No sound of one, perhaps. Richard doesn't believe in giving burglars the chance to escape and break in somewhere else. He would rather catch them red-handed. I thought you would have known that — since you're such a friend.'

An alarm. Gannon could have kicked himself. It had never occurred to him that this place would have an alarm, he hadn't even bothered to look for one, despite the fancy new lock. He could understand the replacement of a lock that had been little more than a joke, but who would put an alarm on an almost derelict fishing cottage, for heaven's sake?

Except it wasn't a derelict fishing cottage any more. It was a warm and welcoming home, occupied by a girl with a face like an angel and the coolness to keep him talking until reinforcements arrived. And he'd thought he had been manipulating her . . .

He covered the distance between them before she could move, taking Sophie from her arms. His ribs complained, but he didn't have time to feel pain. 'You'll forgive me if I don't stop to chat,' he said grimly. 'I assume the front door is still in the same place?'

Dora felt a flutter of anxiety. 'You can't take Sophie out there.' A distant flicker of lightning underscored her words, and the rain began to rattle against the window once more. Anxiety hardened into determination. 'I absolutely forbid it,' she said.

'Oh, really?' If the situation hadn't been so desperate he would have laughed. 'And just how are you going to stop me?'

'Like this.' And she planted herself between him and the door.

Gannon applauded her spirit, but he hadn't got time for games, so he hooked his free arm about her waist and lifted her to one side. Red-hot pain shot through his ribs. He hadn't time for that either. But he staggered slightly as he put her down.

'Oh, good grief, you're hurt — '

'Give the lady a coconut,' he muttered, as he leaned against the wall, waiting for the pain to subside so that he could breathe again.

'Look, don't worry. I'll get rid of them.'

'Oh, really?' he asked harshly. 'And

why would you do that?'

'Heaven knows, but I will. Just stay here and keep quiet.' He stared at her. She lifted her shoulders. It was something between a shimmy and a shrug. It did something to the way her nightgown clung to her slender body that had much the same effect on his breathing as a couple of cracked ribs. She was right, he wasn't going anywhere fast enough to make a difference.

'Whatever you say, lady. Just don't try and be too clever.'

'Clever? Me?' Her mouth suddenly widened in a broad smile. 'You must be joking. I'm just your average dumb blonde.'

Blonde, certainly. A knock 'em dead and wipe the floor with 'em blonde. Average? Scarcely. Dumb? Never. As she turned, with a little switch of her backside as if to prove her point, there was a second, more urgent knock.

'Be careful what you say,' he ordered quietly from the kitchen door, still not sure why he was trusting her.

Dora looked back. Gannon and Sophie were framed in the doorway, and he had his hand stuck in his pocket as if fingering a concealed weapon. Surely not? He was just trying to frighten her . . . Maybe she should be frightened. A whole lot more frightened than she was.

She swallowed as her nerves caught up with her, then spun round, slipped the chain on the door and opened it a crack.

The young constable waiting on the step was little more than a boy, his face so smooth that he didn't look old enough to shave. The idea of asking him to collar a man like Gannon and march him off to the local police station was plainly ridiculous, she told herself. Just in case she needed convincing. Besides, the wretched man would go as soon as he'd rested. And she was quite sure he'd be only too happy to leave Sophie behind if he thought she was in good hands.

'Are you all right, Mrs Marriott?' the

young constable asked, assuming that she was Poppy. She considered correcting his mistake, but decided against it. She wanted him to go as quickly as possible, and that would just slow things down.

'Fine.' The word came out as little more than a croak. 'Fine,' she repeated, more convincingly. 'Why? What's up?'

'Probably nothing, but your security company alerted us that your alarm had been triggered. I'm sorry it took so long to get here, but they're going off all over the place tonight with this storm.'

She worked very hard at keeping her smile in place, her expression showing nothing more than mild surprise.

'I've looked around, but everything seems secure.' The constable glanced up. 'Your security lights don't seem to be working, though.'

'No, I turned them off,' she said, cursing herself for all kinds of a fool. If they'd been on they might have deterred her unwanted visitor. Except where would little Sophie be now?

Soaked to the skin beneath some hedge. A prime candidate for pneumonia.

She reached for the switch and the area around the cottage was floodlit for a hundred feet, illuminating a police car parked a few yards away and picking up the rain spots soaking into the policeman's jacket.

'They seem to light up every time something bigger than a mouse walks by. It makes me jumpy,' she told him, and added a suggestion of a giggle at her own foolishness.

She was careful to keep any special emphasis out of her voice, careful not to do or say anything that might cause the man behind her to lose his nerve and bolt with Sophie into the darkness. Not that there appeared to be anything wrong with his nerves. But still, she wasn't taking any chances.

'Would you like me to come in and check the cottage for you, just in case?' the young man offered.

He took a step forward but she didn't unhook the chain. 'There's no need, really.'

'It wouldn't be any trouble — '

'Pete?' his partner called from the patrol car. 'If you've finished, we've got another call.'

'I'll be right with you.' Pete turned back to her. 'As I said, it was probably the lightning that set off the alarm, Mrs Marriott.' He nodded towards the car. 'I expect this is another one.'

'How trying for you. I'm terribly sorry that you've had a wasted journey.'

'No problem. Just get the alarm checked out in the morning.' He glanced up again. 'And keep the lights on. They do make opportunist thieves think twice.'

Too late for that. 'I'll do that,' she assured him. 'And thank you for coming to check up on me.'

'It's what we're here for. Goodnight, ma'am.'

She could scarcely believe that she was letting him walk away. What on earth was she thinking of? She ought to call him back —

'Shut the door, Mrs Marriott. Now.'

33

Gannon's voice was barely audible from the other side of the door. Too late. She pushed it shut and turned to lean against it as her legs buckled a little at her own stupidity. 'I can't believe I just did that.'

'Don't worry. You played the dumb blonde so well that the poor kid will break his neck to get back and check up on you the minute that lightning and burglar alarms permit. I'll just have to rely on the fact that you're a respectable married lady who will swiftly send him about his business.'

Married? For a moment Dora couldn't think what John Gannon was talking about, then she realised he had picked up on the young policeman's mistake. She glared at him. It was what any respectable married lady would do under the circumstances, wasn't it?

Who was she kidding? Under the circumstances any respectable married lady would have screamed the place down, not offered a burglar the comfort of her home.

'We'll see. If you're really such a good friend of Richard's, I've got nothing to fear.' She stared pointedly at his hand, still in his pocket. 'Have I?'

'No, Mrs Marriott,' he said, taking his hand carefully from his jacket pocket and pulling the lining out with it, to show her that it was quite empty. 'Nothing at all.' The truth of the matter was that Gannon, his ribs giving him hell, his shoulder protesting at the weight of Sophie as she slumped against him, felt incapable of raising a sweat on a nervous fly. And he had no wish to frighten her; what he wanted was her help. 'Besides, if I hurt you, Richard would probably hunt me down and kill me with his bare hands.'

Dora didn't anticipate raising that kind of passion in Richard for herself, but she had a pretty good idea of what he would do to anyone who even considered hurting her sister. And, because her intruder had picked up the policeman's mistake, he was now under the impression that she was Richard's wife. Well, if that impression was going to keep her safe, she wasn't about to disabuse him.

'Only *probably*, you think?'

He met her gaze head on, for a moment meeting her challenge. Then there was the tiniest contraction of lines fanning out from his eyes, softening his face in an oddly seductive smile that made her catch at her breath. 'No, not probably, Mrs Marriott. Without question.' And his voice, back to silken velvet, did nothing to help.

She swallowed hard. 'I'm glad you realise that,' she said, with commendable briskness under the circumstances. 'Now, if you're staying, hadn't you better give Sophie her milk?' He glanced down at Sophie, but she had finally fallen asleep across his shoulder and Dora's heart went out to the little girl. 'Poor soul. Look, why don't you take her upstairs and tuck her up in my bed? I'll bring up the milk. In case she wakes,' she added.

His smile deepened slightly. 'Whilst I

admire your initiative and appreciate your kindness, I think we'll revert to me giving the orders and you carrying them out. I feel safer that way.' He eased Sophie gently away from his shoulder, his expression tender as he placed the child into Dora's arms, brushed a strand of hair back from her face. She didn't stir. Then he looked up and caught Dora's thoughtful expression. 'You might have sent the police about their business, but I'm sure you must have plans to call for reinforcements of some kind. Plans that involve using a telephone?'

Dora hadn't given the telephone a thought — not that she'd had an opportunity to use it even if she had. Well, he might have wildly over-estimated her ability to think on her feet, but it wasn't too late to start doing just that. Richard's sister lived a couple of miles away with her husband. They would know exactly what to do in a situation like this. 'Perhaps I have,' she said, rewarding him with a smile for such cleverness. 'I suppose you'll want to disconnect it?'

He considered the matter. He would need a telephone if he was going to sort out Sophie's papers, make things right with the authorities, but he couldn't do that tonight, and this woman was too much of an unknown quantity to risk leaving it connected. 'I suppose I will.'

'It's in the living room,' she informed him, as he poured the warm milk into a mug. 'Please try not to make a mess of the wall when you yank it out. It's only just been decorated.'

The last thing he wanted to do was yank it out of the wall. 'Find me a screwdriver and I'll reconnect it before I leave,' he promised. 'Are there any extensions upstairs?'

'None. Although I'm sure you'll insist on checking for yourself.'

'Oh, yes, I'll check.' Gannon's grin was unexpected, deepening the lines carved into his cheeks, sparking his warm brown eyes with golden flecks of light, lifting one corner of his mouth as if self-mockery was second nature to him. 'Although I can understand Richard's unwillingness to install a telephone in the bedroom. If you were my wife I wouldn't have a telephone within twenty miles of the place.'

Dora, usually capable of putting down a flirtatious male at thirty paces, with one hand tied behind her back, for a moment floundered helplessly while her brain scrambled to formulate an appropriate response. But nothing had prepared her for an encounter with a man like Gannon. There was a predatory edge to him that stirred the tiny hairs on the nape of her neck, warning her that he would do anything to get what he wanted. And a little part of her that thought she might rather like it.

'How fortunate that I'm not,' she replied, as coldly as she could. Somehow it didn't sound cold, just a little breathless. Not very convincing. She tried again. 'Just think how inconvenient it would be not to have a telephone.'

'I'd consider it worth any amount of inconvenience to have you all to myself, Mrs Marriott. Without interruption.'

Now that *was* convincing. The man could give lessons in the subject. It was a long time since anyone had managed to bring Dora to blushing point, but the heat tingling along her cheekbones was unmistakable. John Gannon might not have shaved for two days, but somehow, when he smiled, it was very easy to forget that fact.

She was sure now that he had no intention of hurting her. But he was still a dangerous man.

And every time he called her Mrs Marriott, and she accepted the name, she was taking a convenient misunderstanding and turning it into a lie. 'Please don't call me that,' she instructed.

His brows rose slightly at her abruptness. 'Why not? If it's your name?'

She neither confirmed nor denied it. 'Such formality seems a little out of place, don't you think? My name is Pandora. Most people just call me Dora.'

'I'm not most people.'

'No,' she agreed. 'Most people don't break in in the middle of the night and frighten innocent women out of their wits.'

'I'd say that it was debatable who frightened who the most. But perhaps, under the circumstances, we should compromise on Pandora. It wouldn't do to get too familiar.'

'Under what circumstances?'

'Under the circumstances that you're married to my very good friend Richard Marriott,' he said. 'Although for some reason you don't appear to be wearing a wedding ring.'

Definitely dangerous. 'Contrary to popular belief, it's not compulsory,' she said. She knew that wouldn't satisfy him, but she didn't give him a chance to say so. 'I don't remember seeing you at the wedding?' Because he hadn't been there. While she and Poppy bore a strong family resemblance, her sister oozed glamour and poise from every pore. He would never have confused the two of them. 'Oh, no, of course you couldn't have been there. You didn't know Richard had remarried.'

'Big do, was it?'

'Pretty big.' It had been enormous. Richard's status as minor aristocracy guaranteed media interest, and as for Poppy . . . Well anything that Poppy did made the news. But despite the crush she knew that Gannon hadn't been part of it. She wouldn't have forgotten anything as dangerous on two legs as John Gannon. She half turned. 'Why didn't he invite you?'

'I've been abroad for quite a while. Out of touch. When, exactly, was the happy event?'

'At Christmas.'

'At Christmas? Richard must have been seriously good all year if he found you beneath his tree. I really must try a lot harder.'

'Richard doesn't have to try, Mr Gannon. It comes naturally to him.'

Mouth, mouth, mouth. It would get her into trouble if she didn't watch out.

But John Gannon didn't appear to take offence, although it was difficult to tell what he was thinking. That kind of smile could hide a lot. 'You can drop the mister, Pandora. Since we're on first-name terms.'

Dora glared at him. She was damned if she was going to call him John. 'Thank you. Gannon.'

There was an infinitesimal pause. 'Any time.'

'And I really would prefer it if you called me Dora.'

'I'll try and remember that.'

'Did you say you've been abroad?'

'I did,' he confirmed, but didn't elaborate.

'I see.' And as she lay Sophie down in the warm nest of the bed she had so recently vacated, tucked the cover up beneath her chin, Dora quite suddenly thought that maybe she did see. The little girl was dark-haired. Well, so was Gannon — but Sophie's skin had that olive, Mediterranean look about it. She turned to him. 'Have you snatched her?' He stared at her. 'From her mother? This is one of those terrible tug-of-love cases, isn't it?'

She had half expected him to explode at her accusation. He didn't, but appeared interested in her reasoning. 'What makes you think that?' he asked.

'Well, it's perfectly obvious you're not a run-of-the-mill house-breaker, Gannon. You were just looking for somewhere to lie low and you remembered this place, assumed it would be empty.'

'My mistake,' he agreed. 'But Richard would have helped me if he'd been here. When will he be back?'

'You don't know him that well if you believe he'd consider helping you take a child away from her mother,' Dora declared, shocked by the very idea.

'This is not a tug-of-love case, Dora. Richard will help — when he knows the facts.'

'I'm here. Tell *me* the facts, Gannon.'

'Where is he?'

'Richard?' She hesitated. She had been planning to tell him that her brother-in-law was due back at any moment, and that he would do well to make himself scarce before he arrived. But it seemed that Gannon would actually welcome his arrival; if she told him Richard was due back, there was no way he would leave.

She would have to tell him the truth. But not the *whole* truth — that Poppy had gone to the States where she had just landed a contract as the new face of a huge cosmetics company, and that Richard wasn't ready to let his new wife out of his sight.

'I'm sorry, Gannon, but Richard is in the States on business. He won't be back for at least a week,' she compromised. 'You will understand if I don't ask you to stay and wait for him?'

His face tightened. 'I understand perfectly, Dora. But if you don't want me hanging around you're going to have to stand in for him. I need money and I need transport.'

'Transport?' She frowned. She knew something had been bothering her. The policeman hadn't mentioned any suspicious-looking vehicle parked in the lane. 'How did you get here without a car?'

'I walked.'

'Walked! From where?' The nearest major road was miles away. He didn't answer. 'Well, I suppose you can take my car.' He would undoubtedly take it anyway, so she might as well make a virtue of a necessity.

'Thank you.'

Dora stared down at the sleeping child, who hadn't even stirred as she'd been laid in the bed. 'And I can let you have a little cash.' She gave him a sideways glance. 'Or quite a lot, if you'll let me go to the bank.' He shook his head. 'No, I didn't think you'd do that. I suppose I could let you have my cash card.'

'And I suppose you'd tell me the correct number?'

'I would,' she promised. 'I wouldn't want you coming back.' She mentally corrected herself. She wouldn't want him coming back *angry*. There was another reason for convincing him that she was telling the truth. 'But you'll have to leave Sophie with me. She shouldn't be going through all this.' He gave an odd little sigh and she turned to him, sure that she could make him see sense. He was staring down at the sleeping child, his face creased in concern. Then, as if sensing her gaze, he turned to meet it, challenge it. 'I'd look after her, Gannon,' she said, with sudden compassion for the man.

'Would you? For how long?'

It was an odd question. 'Until she can be returned to her mother of course. I'll take her myself, if you like . . . ' She was sure he was wavering. 'I won't say anything to the police.'

'Why not?'

'Because there's nothing to be gained from it.' He was regarding her intently. 'Because you're Richard's friend.' She knew she was being silly, but right at that moment the child was more important than any amount of common sense. 'Does it matter?'

Gannon stared at her strangely familiar face. He'd been running for days, ever since he had grabbed Sophie from the refugee camp. He was hurt, hungry, exhausted, and he'd broken into Richard's cottage in a desperate need for somewhere to hide, somewhere to keep Sophie safe while he recouped his strength, sorted things out. And this woman was offering to help, although she didn't know the first thing about him. More than that, she was looking at him as if her heart would break. Of course it mattered. It shouldn't, but it did.

Or maybe he was so tired that he was just hearing and seeing what he longed for most. Trusting her just because she looked like the angel he needed right now would almost certainly be a mistake. 'I won't be taking her anywhere tonight,' he conceded. 'I'll see how she is in the morning and then I'll decide what to do next.'

'She needs time, Gannon. A chance to recover.'

'And these.' He produced a small bottle of pills from his pocket.

'What are they?' Dora asked suspiciously.

'Just antibiotics.' He sat on the edge of the bed, coaxed the child half awake and persuaded her to swallow a capsule with a little of the milk. She was asleep again before her head hit the pillow. Then he turned and looked up at the girl standing beside him. 'Will you help us, Pandora? Give us a little of your hope?'

The thing that most people remembered about the legend of Pandora was that her curiosity had let loose all the troubles of the world. He remembered that she had given the world hope, too. How could she possibly turn him down?

Dora gave a little gasp, scarcely able to believe how easy it was to be suborned by a pair of warm eyes, by a smile that could break a girl's heart without really trying.

'You ask as if I have a choice,' she

replied, cross at such weakness. Yet she'd already sent the police away. She was already his accomplice, whether she was prepared to admit it or not. Then her glance flickered over the dishevelled appearance of her unwanted guest, the sunken cheeks in his exhausted face, and something inside her softened. She didn't entirely believe him when he said this was not a tug-of-love case, but he must love his daughter, miss her desperately, to have been driven to such lengths.

'You look as if you could do with a drink yourself,' she said. 'Something rather stronger than milk.'

He dragged his hand over his face in an unconscious gesture of weariness. 'You're right; it's been one hell of a day. Thanks.'

'It isn't over yet.' And she'd didn't want his thanks. She just wanted him to do what was right. She crossed to the door, but for a moment John Gannon stayed where he was, a dark, slightly stooped presence, as he leaned over the bed to lift the quilt up over the little girl's shoulders. It was an oddly touching scene, and Dora didn't doubt that he loved the little girl. But she was even more certain that he wasn't telling her the entire truth.

'Shall we go downstairs, where we won't disturb Sophie?' Dora prompted. 'Then you can tell me exactly what is going on.'

★ ★ ★

John Gannon watched the tall, fair-haired girl as she poured a large measure of brandy into a crystal glass. She was heart-stoppingly lovely. When she had stormed into the kitchen with Sophie in her arms, his heart had momentarily stopped. And it hadn't just been because she'd startled him. He'd have felt the same jolt of excitement if he'd seen her from the far side of a crowded room, felt the same heat flooding through his veins. And it made him angry. He had been in too many tight corners to be distracted by a woman, no matter how lovely, when he needed all his wits about him.

But Gannon was angry with Richard, too. Good God, how could he? He liked the man, admired him, but at a guess Dora was scarcely into her twenties — a new-born lamb to Richard's wolf. The man who had once been his champion had become a cynical, hard-bitten misogynist, with one broken marriage behind him and no right . . . no right . . .

He almost laughed out loud at his own self-righteous indignation. He wasn't angry with Richard. He was just plain, old-fashioned jealous. His body was clamouring to take this girl and they were in the classic setting for seduction — alone in a cottage, deep in the most beautiful countryside. And honour dictated that he couldn't make a move on her.

It was probably just as well, under the circumstances. He didn't have the time for dalliance. Or the strength to spare. But it was a pity. This girl had far more than beauty to commend her. She had courage.

Faced with an intruder, anyone might have thrown hysterics, but she'd just been angry with him. Not for breaking in, for heaven's sake, but for taking Sophie out on a wet night. As if he had had any choice.

He could use that kind of courage right now. But so far he hadn't done a very good job of convincing her that he was the kind of man she would want to help. And Richard would never forgive him for involving his pretty new wife in something messy. Not that he was about to underestimate her. He thought Dora might just be the girl to give his kind of problems a run for their money.

Nevertheless, given half a chance to summon assistance, she would undoubtedly take it. And, with that thought uppermost in his mind, he walked across to the telephone and hunkered down to examine the socket. 'How about that screwdriver?' he asked, turning to her.

She was watching him, slate-dark eyes solemn. Then, without a word, she crossed the carpet on those pretty bare feet, the soft silk of the wrap, now tightly fastened about her, clinging to her legs as she walked. 'It's brandy,' she said, as she handed him a glass.

He raised the glass, and raised his brows at the quantity of liquor. 'Enough to lay me low for week,' he said, finding it suddenly a great deal easier to concentrate on the pale amber liquid pooled in the bottom of the glass than meet her silent disapproval.

'Then don't drink it. I can assure you the last thing I want is for you to be here for an entire week.' She looked at the socket. 'Do you have to do that? I'm hardly likely to dial 999, am I? After all, I've already sent the police away.'

'The police, yes. But I'm sure there's someone else you'd like to call. I'll reconnect it before I leave, I promise.' Sooner. But she stood her ground. 'It would be a lot easier just to pull it out of the wall, Dora. You decide.'

Having made her point that the telephone was important, she capitulated. 'There's a screwdriver in the kitchen.'

'Then I suggest you fetch it.' Quickly, before his ribs made the decision for them.

She turned abruptly, her robe stirring the air against his cheek as it swirled round, returning a moment later with a small screwdriver. Then she retreated to the fireplace, kneeling down in front of it so that her hair fell forward over her shoulder, a skein of honeyed silk in the light of a tall lamp that stood on the sideboard beside the drinks tray.

Damn, damn, damn. She was a complication he hadn't bargained on. His life was already loaded with complications, and Richard's empty cottage had seemed the perfect place to hole up while he sorted them out.

As he watched her, she reached for the poker. It was halfway out of the stand when his fingers tightened around her wrist. Startled, she turned to look up at him. 'I'm going to make up the fire,' she protested.

'Are you?' For a moment their eyes clashed, hers stormy grey and about as welcoming as the scudding thunder-clouds that had blacked out the moon as he'd crossed the fields with Sophie whimpering in his arms.

'What else? Laying you out with a poker isn't going to improve things, is it?' she said.

'It would give you time to get help.'

'Oh, right,' she said, looking point-edly at the telephone. 'And how do you suggest I do that? By telepathy?'

'No. You would get in your car and drive away. You did say you had a car, didn't you?' Her wrist was slender, ridiculously slender, the bones delicate, fragile beneath his fingers, stirring the kind of longings that were madness even to contemplate. It had been a long time since he had been this close to a sweet-smelling woman.

He wanted to lower his mouth to the pulse he could feel racketing under the pale skin, taste it, press her palm against his cheek and pull her tight against him to ease the sudden, unexpected ache of longing.

Madness.

3

Madness. Even if she hadn't been Richard Marriott's wife.

As mad as believing that she could wield that great long poker in cold blood and strike him with it. Yet he still relieved her of it with his free hand, before releasing her wrist. Delicate it might be, but he'd been in too many tight spots to take the risk. That was how he'd survived for so long in a dangerous world.

'Well?' he demanded.

Dora didn't bother to answer his question. Instead she rubbed at her wrist, as if to rid herself of his touch, and, thoroughly disgusted with himself and his thoughts, Gannon turned away from her dark, accusing eyes.

'I'll see to the fire,' he said, stirring the ashes with the point of the poker so that the embers pulsed redly.

'Man's work, is it?' she sneered at him. 'And what am I supposed to do? Rush out to the kitchen and rustle you up some food?'

'Thanks for offering, but, no, thanks.' He couldn't remember the last time he had eaten, and his stomach was practically sticking to his backbone, but he had his pride. His stomach, however, had heard the word food and audibly protested. He glanced at the girl beside him and ventured a smile. 'I'm on a diet.' She didn't respond to this olive branch. Quite frankly, he didn't blame her.

He threw some small pieces of stick that had been drying in the basket beside the hearth into the warm embers, and for a moment there was silence as they both watched the wood begin to smoke, then crackle into flame. He added more wood as this sudden application of heat reminded him just how cold he was. August in England. Log fires and thunderstorms. It figured.

Dora, still kneeling on the rug in

front of the hearth, felt rather than heard the shiver run through him. She was still trying to reel in her senses, to recover from what she had seen in his eyes as he had grasped her wrist, to recover from an almost overwhelming urge to put her arms about him and hold him. Except she wouldn't have just held him. What she had seen in his face needed a far deeper comfort than that. Yet she'd made no attempt to pull free, and if he hadn't released her —

'You're wet,' she said, and heard the tiny tremor in her voice.

Gannon turned back to look at her, looking just a moment too long before he switched his gaze to his legs. His jeans, wet to the knees, were beginning to steam in the heat. He'd missed the showers as he'd cut across country, but the grass had been soaking, and, although he'd abandoned his muddy shoes in the kitchen, his socks had left damp marks on the beautiful new carpet.

'It's been raining,' he said, as if this

was sufficient explanation. 'Don't worry about it; I'll dry off in front of the fire.'

'I'm not worried,' she told him. 'But I've got better things to do than nurse a stupid man who sits around in wet clothes and goes down with pneumonia.'

Gannon could think of worse things than being nursed by Pandora Marriott. Somehow he didn't think that saying so would be altogether wise. He shivered again. Why the hell couldn't Richard have found a plain, ordinary girl to love? And if he had to marry someone like Dora, why the hell didn't he stay at home to look after her? She wouldn't have been left on her own for weeks at a time if she'd been *his* woman. No way. As Dora uncurled from the hearth, rising gracefully to her feet, he caught her hand.

'Where are you going?'

'To find something for you to wear.' She was angry with him for touching her again, angry with herself for wanting him to. She tugged at her wrist, but he tightened his grip.

'I'll come with you,' he said, keeping her at his side while he carefully piled logs onto the flames. Then he set the guard in front of the fire. 'You can show me round.'

'Do I have a choice?'

'I'd like to see what you've done to the place since I was last here.' He had avoided a direct answer, she noticed, which was much the same as saying no. And she didn't think he was desperately interested in her sister's talents as an interior decorator either. What he really wanted was to look around and work out the lie of the land. It must have been quite a shock to head for a quiet bolthole only to discover someone had moved in and changed it all.

'And when was that?' she asked.

'Too long ago. Richard invited me down for a few days' fishing before . . . ' He shrugged, apparently unwilling to elaborate.

She didn't press the point. She wasn't interested. *Not much*. 'Well, as a venue for male-bonding on fishing holidays I'm sure it was perfectly adequate. As a family home it had a number of shortcomings — '

'Family? It's a little soon for that, isn't it?'

A second blush seared her cheeks. 'The lack of a bathroom being number one,' she said, determinedly ignoring the way his glance had automatically flicked to her waist.

Unabashed, his golden eyes glinted thoughtfully beneath thick dark lashes as he raised them to her face. 'You mean I won't have to skinny dip in the river?'

'Not unless you want to,' she said crossly. Well, why wouldn't she be cross? With her hand held captive in his, she found it oddly difficult to breathe, and it wasn't just the thought of him swimming naked beneath the huge moon that every once in a while lit up the stormy landscape beyond the living room window. She was cross because, despite the fact that he had broken in, was plainly a bad lot, there was something undeniably appealing about him, especially when he lifted the corner of his mouth in that odd little smile. He was doing it now. 'What's so funny?' she demanded.

'You are. I could read your thoughts then, as clearly as if they were in foot-high letters across your forehead.'

'I very much doubt it.'

'Humour me.' He tapped her forehead with the tip of his finger. 'You were thinking about how much you would enjoy giving me a helping hand into that cold water.'

'Not at all!' Then she gave an awkward little shrug. 'Well, maybe,' she conceded, preferring that he should think that rather than guess what was really going on in her mind. He had discarded his jacket after he had seen Sophie safely in bed, and as she quickly lowered her gaze, just in case her eyes were betraying more than they should, she was confronted with the decidedly grubby Aran sweater he was wearing. It was hand-knitted, and she found herself wondering what woman had given so much of her time, taken so much trouble to keep John Gannon warm. Sophie's mother?

'I'll find you something to wear, and then you can decide whether you prefer a hot shower or a cold dip,' she said, irritated with herself for even wondering about it. 'The choice is entirely yours.' And she pulled her hand free so easily that for a moment she thought she must have imagined the tightness of his grip.

Idiot! she thought as she headed for the stairs. *He wasn't holding your hand like some love-sick boy. To all intents and purposes you're his prisoner, Dora Kavanagh. And don't you forget it.*

As Gannon had immediately realised, the cottage had been extended into part of an old barn, and the master suite was in the new part of the house, with its own bathroom and a dressing room for Poppy. Dora led the way through, pushing open the door to reveal a large bedroom furnished in warm antique pine to keep the cottagey atmosphere. The plush carpet was a soft, misty green and matching velvet curtains were looped back at the windows.

'Wait!' He stopped her as she was about to switch on the light. 'Draw the curtains first.'

She shrugged, did as he ordered without a word, then crossed to Richard's wardrobe. An internal light came on, and she flicked quickly through the shelves before pulling out a sweatshirt and a pair of jogging pants.

She turned to Gannon. 'Will these do?' she asked, holding them out to him.

'Admirably.' He was leaning casually against the architrave, watching her from the doorway. There was something about the way he was looking at her that sent warning shivers up her spine, and it occurred to her that encouraging him to follow her into the bedroom had not been entirely sensible. Except, of course, it would have made no difference. If he'd wanted to come in, he would have. But he stayed where he was.

'You've got plenty of space now,' he said.

There was nothing about his remark that should have concerned her. Yet it did. She threw a nervous glance around the room, wondering if he'd spotted something that had given away her masquerade. A wedding photograph of Poppy and Richard, perhaps. Anything. But there was nothing that she could see.

'I'm glad you approve.' She crossed to him, pushed the clothes into his hands and snapped off the light. She hadn't considered what he might do if he discovered she had been lying to him. It was probably better for her peace of mind to leave it that way. 'The bathroom's this way,' she said. 'I'm sure you could use a shower.' She felt her voice shake. Well, she was supping with the devil; she had a right to be nervous.

'I'm sure I could. But you'll understand if I insist you stay and keep me company.'

'What!'

Gannon discovered that making Dora blush gave him a heady sense of power that he knew was utterly beneath contempt. But she looked so lovely, so delightfully vulnerable . . . 'You'd like me to say that again?' he enquired.

'No!' Then, her cheeks even pinker, 'You can't mean it.'

'I'm afraid I can, and I do.' His regret *might* have been genuine. Somehow Dora doubted it. 'I really can't take the risk that you'll take the opportunity to bolt for it. If the police lock me up, who will look after Sophie?'

'Why would they lock you up?'

'I broke in here; isn't that enough?'

'Not if I don't press charges.'

'Ah, there's the rub. *If.*' She didn't bother to protest that she wouldn't. Why would he believe her? 'You don't have to share the shower with me, Dora. I simply want you to stay near enough to chat. So I know you're there. That's all.'

'*All?*' She almost exploded with rage.

How dared he? For heaven's sake, she might have really been Richard's wife . . . 'Aren't you concerned about Richard's reaction to such a plan?' she said, suddenly latching onto the thought, certain that it would make him think twice.

'He would do the same in my position. He'll understand.' He might have thought twice, but his conclusion was identical.

'Will he?' Her voice came out as little more than a squeak. Apparently he wasn't as bothered by the threat of her brother-in-law as she had hoped. 'And just how understanding would you be?'

'If you were my wife?' He reached out and touched her cheek with the tips of his cold fingers. In the quiet still of the night she couldn't be certain if there had been a flash of lightning outside in the darkness or whether it was electricity flowing straight from his fingers into her body. She held her breath, waiting for the thunder. None came. She wanted to move away, knew she should move away, but was transfixed by the fire in his eyes. 'If you were my wife, Dora, I'd beat him to a pulp,' he said. His hand fell to his side. '*Then* I'd be understanding. Maybe.'

Released from his touch, she finally managed to find her voice. 'I see.' She gave an odd, slightly shaky laugh. 'Well, that's reassuring.'

'Is it?'

'Oh, yes.' Her heartbeat was beginning to return to something resembling normality. 'I'll hold onto the thought that at some time in the future you're going to suffer extreme pain.'

He sketched that oddly disturbing little smile. 'Anything to make you happy. Now, which way did you say the bathroom was?'

Utterly lost for words, she didn't make any further attempt to argue with the man. He'd just demonstrated his ability to be utterly ruthless. She didn't for one moment doubt that he knew Richard, but it had just occurred to her that she only had his word for it that they were friends. Richard might not take the same point of view. Which might just be why he had insisted on disconnecting the telephone.

After all, if she *had* been married to Richard, calling him would have been her first thought, wouldn't it? Surely, if he was the friend he had purported to be, Gannon would have suggested it?

'It's this way,' she said, and without waiting to be ordered in she led the way. 'I hope the decor is equally to your liking. Since you appear to be so interested.'

It was a beautiful bathroom, roomy, warm, with deep fuchsia-red walls and carpet to set off the dark wood of the door and the fittings, the crisp whiteness of the suite. There was a huge, squashy armchair, a table laden with exotic plants and a pile of glossy magazines, and on the walls, in gilt frames that glowed against the rich colour of the paint, a series of botanical prints. It was a bathroom to relax in, to share, if you were so inclined. Gannon glanced around, then nodded towards the chair. 'At least you'll have somewhere comfortable to sit.'

'Thanks,' she said, deeply sarcastic, lowering herself into the armchair, refusing to be embarrassed. There was nothing embarrassing about a naked man, for heaven's sake. And, since she was standing in for Poppy, she would do what her sophisticated big sister would undoubtedly do if she were put in the same impossible position. Sit back and enjoy the show.

She stared up at him, unblinking. He didn't move. 'Don't mind me,' she invited. Then, 'There's plenty of hot water.' It was getting harder to sustain her relaxed demeanour. She managed it just, waving airily in the direction of towels heaped up on glass shelves. 'And towels.' He didn't look away. 'You'll find shampoo . . . ' She faltered as he caught hold of the bottom of his sweater and pulled it, together with the T-shirt he had been wearing beneath it, over his head it one fluid movement and dropped them in a heap on the floor. She stared open-mouthed at the dark bruises that coloured his ribs and shoulder, the scar that puckered the skin of his arm.

'Shampoo?' he prompted.

'On the shelf in the shower stall,' she finished slowly.

The shabbiness of his clothes had not disguised Gannon's quiescent strength. Dora had been toe-tinglingly aware of it from the moment she had set eyes on him, and now, stripped to the waist, the potent power of his lean, bone-hard body more than lived up to that promise.

There wasn't an ounce of excess weight on him. He was pared-to-the-bone thin, his square, wide shoulders arrowing down to a taut midriff that left room to spare in the waistband of his jeans, as if he had been expending more energy than he had been taking in for too long. And if she reached out to run her hand over his ribcage, she knew she would be able to count his battered ribs. One by one.

'You're hurt,' she said, stating the obvious. 'Did you pile up your car? Is Sophie hurt?' She half rose.

'Sit down, Dora. Relax. Sophie is fine and my ribs will heal in their own good time.'

'Will they?' She wasn't so sure. 'Shouldn't you go to the hospital? I'd drive you — '

'I'm sure you would.'

'I didn't mean . . . I wasn't trying to . . . '

'Of course you were, Dora.' His eyes mocked her. 'And I don't blame you. But believe me, all that's needed to heal cracked ribs is time. I speak from experience.'

'Oh.' She subsided into the chair as he reached for his belt.

Dora had been so sure that he would be disconcerted by her boldness — too embarrassed to strip off in front of his friend's new wife. She had been so sure that he would send her packing, giving her a few precious moments of freedom in which to use her mobile phone to call Sarah, Richard's sister. It occurred to her that if Gannon was telling the truth Sarah would almost certainly know him.

But Gannon slipped the leather belt strap through the feeder, pulling it clear of the restraining tooth, and the clink of his buckle mocked her. *Embarrassed? Him?* What a joke.

He flipped open the top button of his jeans and she felt sweat bead her top lip. How far would he go before he turned away? He tugged on the worn brass buttons of his fly. They slipped open easily, and she nervously ran the tip of tongue over her dry lips. For a moment he held them, then she physically jumped as he let go and the jeans collapsed about his ankles with a clatter of buttons and belt. He stepped out of them and bent to hook off his socks.

Then, as he began to straighten, he caught his breath as pain jagged through him. She felt it too, and her hand reached out in an uncertain, half supplicating little gesture. She wanted to help, but did not know how, and when his gaze intercepted hers she could see that the character lines were etched more deeply into his cheeks, about his mouth, as if the pain were a knife, carving into the flesh. And his eyes were agate-hard as he struggled to keep from crying out.

'You can close your eyes, Dora,' he muttered, his face inches from hers. 'I didn't say you had to watch.' He wasn't going to back down. No way. 'And I'm big enough to undress myself.' She snatched back her hand. He didn't want her help. Not this kind of help, anyway. 'In your own time,' he prompted, and slowly straightened until he was standing absolutely upright, before hooking his thumbs in the top of his underpants to expose the line where darkly tanned skin suddenly became startlingly white.

Dora slammed her lids down and kept them that way until she heard the shower door click into place, the hiss of water.

'Talk to me, Dora,' he called. 'I want to know you're there.'

'I've got nothing to say to you.'

'Then sing.'

Sing? Was the man crazy? He expected her to sing to him? 'You're the one in the shower. You sing,' she told him.

The sound of the water stopped abruptly, and the door slid partly back. His dark hair, long and shaggy and in desperate need of a cut, was curling damply at his neck. 'I thought we'd agreed that I give the orders, Dora. You sing, or you get in here with me.'

'Can I keep my clothes on?'

He glowered at her. 'You *can* sing, can't you?'

She almost smiled at that. Her inability to carry a tune was legendary within the family. But if he could stand it she certainly could, and she began to sing, putting every ounce of feeling into lyrics of the only song that seemed suitable to sing to a would-be kidnapper, 'Please Release Me.'

He glared at her briefly, then slammed the shower door shut. As the noise of the water drowned her out, he shouted, 'Louder!'

She obliged, entering into the spirit of the song with such gusto that she didn't realise for a moment that the water had stopped. 'When you've quite finished, could you pass me a towel?'

About to tell him to get it himself, she realised that would mean he would have to step naked from the shower stall. She didn't kid herself that he would be in the least bit bothered by that. He was thinking of her — or more probably of Richard. She leapt from the chair and grabbed a towel, thrusting it at him at the full stretch of her arm.

'Thank you,' he said, and the corner of his mouth kinked up again, as if he knew exactly what was driving such instant obedience.

A few moments later he emerged from the shower stall, wrapped modestly from waist to ankle in a dark red bathsheet. He took another towel from the pile and began to dry his hair, favouring his left side.

'Tell me, Dora, where did you learn to sing that badly?' he asked.

'Learn?'

'No one could sing so consistently off-key without lessons.'

'I guess it must be a gift,' she said.

'Then allow me to tell you that you're very gifted indeed.' He gave her a sideways glance. 'What *do* you do? Or perhaps I should say what *did* you do, before you began playing house with Richard? How did you meet him?'

'My sister introduced us,' she said, truthfully enough. 'And playing house keeps me busy. Especially when I have uninvited guests. Do you want to borrow a razor?'

He rubbed his hand over his chin and peered into the mirror. He was clearly unhappy with what he saw. 'Yours?' he asked doubtfully.

She refused to be goaded. 'I'm sure

you'd be more comfortable with Richard's. Since you're such old friends.'

'I assumed he had taken his with him.' She hadn't thought of that.

'He might have a spare.'

'Don't you know?' She might have, if she'd been his wife. Yet somehow she couldn't see Poppy bothering about such things. Her sister definitely wasn't the housewifely type, but then Richard hadn't married her for her domestic achievements. She headed for the door, but his hand reached over her head and kept her from opening it.

'Where do you think you're going?'

'To fetch it from Richard's . . . ' She swallowed. 'From our . . . ' She just couldn't look him in the eye and say it. 'I won't be a minute. Or maybe you'd rather grow a beard to disguise yourself?'

'No,' he said. 'I don't need a disguise.'

'Really? That's just as well. It wouldn't suit you.' She indicated the door and waited for him to open it. 'I'll keep singing, if you like, so that you can keep tabs on me.'

'Please do, but quietly, so that you don't wake Sophie. Just . . . change the record.'

'Don't you like it?' She didn't wait for his answer, but disappeared through the doorway, still singing the same wretched song, but softly.

Despite himself, Gannon smiled.

Dora continued to hum and sing tunelessly as she searched through Richard and Poppy's bathroom cupboards, finding, to her relief, a razor, a pot of shaving soap and an old-fashioned shaving brush.

Then, humming a little louder as she moved down the landing, she sped back to her own room where Sophie was still fast asleep. Her mobile phone was in her handbag, and she had the feeling that sooner or later Gannon would raid it. For money, or credit cards, or her car keys. She retrieved the phone, and was just about to turn it on when she became aware of Gannon's shadow falling across the bed.

'What are you doing?'

Dora had known he was there, but she still jumped guiltily and swung round to face him, hands behind her back. 'You startled me.'

'You stopped singing.'

'Yes.' Her heart was racketing like a runaway tram as she stuffed the telephone beneath the covers. 'I . . . um . . . thought I heard Sophie crying. It would be too bad if I disturbed her with my top C,' she said, with a shaky little laugh.

'You haven't got a top C,' he responded. 'And was she?' He was wearing Richard's jogging pants but nothing else, and up close in the dim light that spilled through the doorway he seemed far more dangerous than when he had stripped off in the bright bathroom.

He looked around her at the sleeping child. 'Crying?' he prompted.

'No. It must have been the wind.' She was glad he wasn't looking at her, or he would have known she was lying. He glanced back at her, and she was certain he knew anyway, but he didn't say anything, simply stepped around her and bent over Sophie, settling the covers over her where she had pushed them away. Dora held her breath as he began to tuck in the bottom sheet. He must see the phone, surely? Or Sophie would wake and feel it.

'Her flush seems to have gone,' Dora said, hoping to distract him. She touched the back of her fingers lightly against Sophie's forehead. 'Do you think she's cooler?'

Gannon abandoned the sheet to touch the child's temple with his fingers, and he nodded. 'She just needs rest, a chance to recover.'

'And she'll get that racing about the countryside in a thunderstorm in the dead of night with you?' she said, hoping that attack would be the most effective form of defence.

'No. That's why I brought her here,' he replied, turning to her. 'Well, where is it?'

She froze. 'What?'

'The razor?'

The razor. Her guilty thoughts had still been locked on the mobile phone, and she'd barely managed to stop herself from looking down at the bed, where she was certain it must be making a lump a foot high. She'd forgotten all about Richard's shaving gear.

'It's here.' Beside her bag on the night table. She picked it up. 'I'll bring it now.' She started for the door, anxious to get him out of the bedroom before he noticed that the bottom sheet was still sticking out untidily and decided to do something about it. But he stopped her.

'It's all right, Dora. I can handle things from here.' He took the bowl of soap, the razor and the brush from her. The back of his hand brushed against the silk, against the swell of her breast, and she jumped as if stung. If he noticed, he didn't let it show. 'There's no reason why you shouldn't get back to sleep now.'

She gaped at him. 'You expect me to go back to sleep?' *He had to be kidding.* 'You've got to be kidding,' she said.

He offered a smile. 'So long as you behave yourself you'll be quite safe, I promise. But, since Sophie has taken your bed, stay with her if it makes you feel less vulnerable.'

'Don't you want to stay with her?'

'I'm sure you'll take good care of her, Dora. I'll stretch out on the sofa downstairs.' He was in no hurry to leave, though, and, reaching behind her, he picked up her handbag. 'But you won't mind if I take this with me, will you? Just as a precaution.'

She shook her head wordlessly. How easily she could have lost her only contact with the outside world if she hadn't taken a chance when it offered . . .

No. She mouthed the word, but no sound came out. 'No,' she repeated. 'Help yourself.'

'I hope I don't have to. But if I do, I'll leave an IOU for anything that I take.'

'Great,' she said, with an airy gesture. 'No problem. Take anything you want.' He could help himself to the kitchen sink just as long as he went. Dora was quite sure her sister would understand, and Gannon could explain himself to Richard when he caught up with him.

She glanced at the bed. Dora had put the idea of sleep on indefinite hold, but at least if she stayed with the child Gannon couldn't sneak off with her. And once he had gone downstairs she would be able to rescue her telephone and summon help.

Don't look at the bed.

'Would you like me to tuck you in?' he asked, in no hurry to leave. 'Since Richard isn't here?'

Dora felt her cheeks heat up. Blushing was getting to be a serious problem. 'I think I can manage that for myself. Thanks all the same. Will you close the door on your way out?' He didn't move. 'Please?' He shrugged and headed for the door, but turned in the opening.

'Do you like tea first thing, or coffee?' She let out an explosive little sound. 'I'm just trying to be a considerate house guest.'

'The most considerate thing you can do is leave. Now.'

'I'm sorry, Dora. I can't be that considerate. Sophie needs a good night's sleep.'

'Then why don't you go and leave us *both* in peace? I'll look after Sophie.'

'Will you?' For a long moment their eyes clashed. 'We come as a package deal, Dora. You can't have one without the other; try and separate us and you'll find that I'm more trouble than you can handle.' Then he closed the door and left her in the dark.

Ain't that the truth, she thought. She might have sent away the police, but she needed some kind of help to get her out of this mess. Well, Sarah came from a long line of women who had spent their lives organising the Empire. She would know exactly what to do.

She leaned over the edge of the bed

and reached carefully beneath the mattress for the telephone, holding her breath as Sophie stirred in her sleep. One murmur from the little girl and Gannon would be back.

Her fingers brushed against the hard casing and she grasped it, pulled it out, and with a hand that shook rather more than she had realised pressed the button to switch it on.

Nothing.

She tried again.

Still nothing. The battery was quite flat.

4

Gannon closed the door, his fingers still tingling where they had brushed against the smooth satin covering her breast. What the hell was the matter with him?

He'd spent his thirtieth birthday in a snow-filled fox-hole being fired on by snipers, for heaven's sake. He was too old, he'd seen too much to be jumping like a teenager just because his hand had come into contact with a warm female and provoked an obvious, if unexpected, response in her.

But one thing was certain: Dora was not like any newly-wed he'd ever met. At least not any happy one. And it was hardly the action of a besotted groom to go away, leaving his new wife behind. Had she, he wondered, moved out of the marital bedroom before or after Richard had gone? Before, he decided. No woman would have left a room she had decorated for herself unless driven from it. His jaw tightened.

Then there was the way she had looked at him while he stripped off in the bathroom. He'd assumed she would stay on the other side of the door. It was all he had intended. Yet she had swept into that bathroom as if she couldn't wait, staring at him with those incredible eyes. For a moment he had been tempted to take her up on what he'd seen there. Even with a couple of cracked ribs he had been hard pressed to stop himself, and to hell with honour.

On top of everything was the disconcerting feeling that he'd met her before somewhere. But how on earth could he have forgotten a girl who looked at him with eyes like black diamonds, eyes that made his body feel too tight for his skin?

The thought of being enfolded in the arms of a tender, sweet-smelling woman and just held for a while was almost irresistible, and she was there for the taking; he knew it. He stared at the bedroom door. Just a few centimetres of wood was all that stood between them.

Then, furious with himself for what he was thinking, he turned and strode back down the landing. If he had any sense he'd keep right on going. But sense didn't come into it. There was Sophie to consider.

He would have turned around and left if it had been possible, the minute he had discovered the cottage wasn't empty. But, tough as she was, Sophie couldn't take much more, and he was all that stood between her and the horrors he had snatched her from. She would be safe at the cottage for a day or two. It wouldn't take the authorities much longer than that to discover the whereabouts of the plane he'd borrowed, and his inelegant landing in a field would be altogether too interesting for the papers to ignore. He just hoped it was long enough.

He pushed open the bathroom door and dumped the shaving gear along with Dora's bag into the sink, then clutched the edge of the basin as a sudden wave of nausea hit him. He was so damned tired. Hungry too, but the tiredness was worse. That was why he had made such a hash of landing the plane.

He eased his aching shoulder and stared at his reflection in the mirror, scarcely recognising himself. He was just as much in need of time to recover as Sophie. If he could get a few hours' sleep he'd be able to think more clearly, sort something out.

He stared down at Dora's bag. It wasn't one of those neat little jobs, made to carry nothing but a wallet, a comb and a lipstick. It was a roomy carry-all, the kind that women stuff all their worldly belongings into and take everywhere with them. He picked it up, forcing himself to open it and turn it out onto the table.

Relief almost overwhelmed him. For a moment, when she had suddenly gone quiet, stopped singing that awful song, he'd had a terrible suspicion that she might have a mobile phone tucked away somewhere. Not that she'd had time to use it, but he was getting careless. The possibility should have occurred to him when she'd made so little fuss about disconnecting the telephone.

At the time he'd assumed she was being pragmatic, but he was beginning to suspect that Dora didn't know the meaning of the word.

He regarded the contents of her bag with a certain bemusement. There was a lifetime of receipts — everything from supermarket till roll to a detailed handwritten account from a London design house. His brows rose at the amount. It seemed inconceivable that one woman could possibly spend that much on clothes.

There was a programme for a production of *Twelfth Night* in the open air at some stately home, and a wallet with sixty-five pounds, some loose change, enough classy charge cards to affect the balance of payments and a driving licence, all in the name of Dora Kavanagh. Surely she should have altered them to her married name by now? Or was she one of those modern women who preferred to use their own name?

Kavanagh? Something on the edge of his memory stirred, and then slipped away. He shook his head. It would come sooner if it wasn't forced.

He picked up a small diary. She was a busy girl. He flipped through one or two pages. Mostly lunch dates at expensive restaurants, occasional weeks blocked out with a vertical line, suggesting unavailability. He tossed it back on the pile, disgusted with himself for even opening it. All he had been interested in was the possibility of a telephone.

Apart from that there was the usual clutter of makeup, hairpins and car keys. He pocketed the car keys and, after a moment's hesitation, the money, then scooped the contents back into the bag.

No phone. He had been lucky, he knew, but it was a mistake he wouldn't normally have made. And if he didn't get out of this chair right now, he'd make another one by falling asleep.

He hauled himself to his feet and began to run hot water, forcing himself to shave even though his hands were beginning to shake with exhaustion. He might have to leave in a hurry, and a scruffy man always attracted more attention than a neat one. Before he left, he'd help himself to some clean clothes from Richard's wardrobe. His wife wasn't likely to object; he had a suspicion that Dora wouldn't even notice. She'd had to hunt for the tracksuit.

He dried his face, held his breath while he went through the painful process of pulling on the sweatshirt, then dragged his fingers through his hair. It needed cutting, badly, but there was nothing he could do about that.

He had intended to peek in the bedroom as he passed, check on Sophie and replace the bag on the chest of drawers. But as he approached the door it was standing wide open, and, although Sophie was fast asleep, just where he had left her, Dora had gone.

Gannon took the stairs three at a time without even feeling the pain jarring his ribs, expecting the back door to be standing wide open as she made a crazy dash to get away from him, but in the living room everything was as it should be.

The fire was crackling behind the guard, throwing a warm, flickering light in a semicircle that included the two chairs placed beside it. Dora was curled up in one of them, her head bent over a lined notepad, her fair hair gleaming in the pool of light from an angled lamp. She didn't even look up as he burst into the room.

'What are you doing?' he demanded. 'I thought you were going to stay with Sophie.' He was aware that he was making a fool of himself. 'Get some sleep,' he finished, somewhat lamely.

She shifted slightly, bit the end of her pen. 'I couldn't sleep. It's the thunder. That's why I got up in the first place.'

'You're scared of thunder?' He was surprised. She was willow-slender, but there was a whipcord strength about her. She didn't seem the kind of girl to be frightened of anything.

'No. It doesn't scare me.' She finally looked up. 'It just brings back unpleasant memories. Things I'd rather not think about. If I work, it helps to block it out.'

'I see.'

'You don't, but it doesn't matter.' She regarded him steadily for a moment with those big dark eyes, then she turned away and picked up a mug at her elbow. She saw that he was still staring at her. 'It's cocoa,' she said. 'I would have made you some, but in your position I wouldn't trust me not to dope it with sleeping pills or something.'

'You wouldn't do that,' he said, responding more easily to teasing hostility. 'You're too eager for me to clear out.'

'True. But, since you don't seem very keen to go, drugging you and getting someone else to carry you away would be a very neat alternative. And far more sensible than attempting to brain you with a poker. However, since I don't take sleeping pills, you're quite safe. Would you like something to eat? There's some unopened cheese in the fridge, or eggs. They'd be safe. And you brought your own milk.' She put down the mug and started to make a note on the pad in front of it. 'Where did you buy it at this time of night?' He didn't answer. 'The only place I know is the all-night garage on the main road.' She stopped writing and looked up at him in astonishment. 'You've walked that far? With Sophie?'

'Just a stroll,' he assured her.

No snipers, no landmines, no missiles. A piece of cake. He glanced at the chair opposite her and, after a moment of hesitation, sat down. 'What are you doing?'

'I'm writing,' she said.

He could see that. 'A letter, a poem, a plea for help that you plan to put in a bottle and fling into the river in the hope that some early morning fisherman might find it?'

'No. Actually, it's an article for a women's magazine.'

'Oh.' Dora had taken the wind out his sails and had rather enjoyed the experience. 'You're a writer? Are you successful?'

'Are you asking if I make a lot of money?'

'Do you?'

She could have told him that she had no need to do anything for money. She could have told him that newspapers and magazines had besieged her for her story and that she'd decided to tell it in order to publicise her cause. But she didn't want him that interested. 'Not yet.'

She could see by his switched off expression that he thought she was kidding herself. And he was slipping further down into the chair as the heat made him sleepy.

Gannon squeezed his eyes tight, pinching the bridge of his nose between his finger and thumb as he fought his body's urge to sleep. Food would help. 'I think I'll take you up on that offer of something to eat,' he said.

'Help yourself.' She jotted something down on the pad, as if it was of no interest to her whether he ate or not. 'You look as if you haven't had a square meal for a week.'

'I haven't.'

'Really?' She finally gave him her full attention. 'You do look absolutely terrible.'

'Thanks, but I had noticed. I'm not feeling particularly great either, if you're interested.'

She leaned forward, as if she might reach out to him. But she kept her hands on the pad in her lap. 'Look, if you'll trust me not to poison you, I'm quite willing to cook something for you.' He regarded her for a moment. While he was sure she wasn't going to poison him, he wasn't prepared to trust her much further than that. 'Just some bacon and eggs, perhaps?'

'An early breakfast?'

'If you like.' She uncurled from the chair and dropped the pad and pencil on the table beside her. 'It won't take long. Why don't you try that drink? It might help.'

His untouched glass stood on the table beside him. He picked it up, sipped the liquor and felt its heat seep down inside him. It felt good. Too good. He put the glass down and pushed himself to his feet. She looked round as he followed her into the kitchen. 'I'll give you a hand.'

She shrugged, as if she wasn't bothered. But it suited her just fine. Anything to keep him downstairs. 'The fridge is over there.'

He crossed to the refrigerator and scanned the shelves, taking out orange juice, a box of eggs and an unopened packet of bacon.

Dora took down a pan and set it on

the hob while Gannon opened the packet of bacon she had bought that morning and piled it in. She smothered a yawn and looked at the clock. It was nearly three. She corrected herself. *Yesterday* morning. And that was the last time she had used the mobile phone.

She had been waiting for a call and had left it switched on in her bag when she had dashed to the supermarket. And now it was as flat as a pancake. She poured out a couple of glasses of juice and sipped one. How on earth could she have been so stupid?

Easily, was the simple answer. She did it all the time. And any other time it wouldn't have mattered.

She'd put it in the charger beside her bed, and pushed it as far out of sight as she could. But she knew Gannon would keep a close eye on her, and he would be less likely to discover her secret if she kept him away from the bedroom.

It wouldn't take long to put some life back into the battery, and once Gannon had some food inside him, and she'd made up the fire, she was certain it wouldn't be very long before he fell asleep. But she knew he was more likely to co-operate if he thought it was his idea.

'There are some mushrooms if you fancy them.' She crossed to the fridge and took them from the cooler.

'Field mushrooms,' he said, looking over her shoulder. 'Where did you get them?'

'I picked them this morning.' He glanced at her thoughtfully, and she knew exactly what he was thinking. 'I'll eat one myself if you like,' she offered.

'That won't be necessary. I'm quite capable of spotting a mistake. Deliberate or otherwise.' She put them on the centre island and began to break eggs into a bowl. Gannon slid onto a stool opposite her. 'How did you meet Richard?' he asked.

She kept her eyes on the bowl, wishing that she had never started this stupid deception. Her sigh was unconscious, but heartfelt. 'I told you, my sister introduced us,' she replied, giving herself time to come up with something convincing while she beat the eggs.

'He's not much of a party-goer.' She didn't offer any help. 'He met his first wife on a shoot.'

'I don't shoot.'

'No.' Her skin, with its delicate peach bloom, had none of the weathered look of a dedicated outdoors enthusiast.

'How's the bacon?' she asked.

He crossed to the cooker and checked the pan. 'Fine.' He threw in a handful of mushrooms and continued to regard her thoughtfully while she poured the eggs into a small saucepan and joined him. 'All right, I give up. Tell me.'

'It was through work.' Dora was glad she had to concentrate on the eggs. She had decided it would be easier to stick to Poppy's story than invent one of her own. But she didn't have to like it.

'Your sister worked for him?'

Actually her sister had been working on a photographic shoot for some outdoorsy make-up ads on the river.

'Not exactly — '

'Sophie! What's the matter?'

Dora turned and saw the little girl standing in the doorway. Something about the way she was fidgeting provoked sympathetic memories. 'I think she needs the bathroom, Gannon. Do you want me to deal with it?'

'No. She doesn't know you. And she doesn't speak much English.' He bent and picked the child up. Dora, watching from a distance, could have sworn that sweat started on his forehead as he bit down on the pain. The child muttered something to him, but he shook his head and without a word carried her across the living room before disappearing into the front hall.

They were gone for some time. Dora was just beginning to wonder if he'd fallen asleep beside the child, after he'd put her back to bed, when they both reappeared.

Sophie was wearing a clean T-shirt that came down to her feet, and a thick cardigan that trailed behind her.

'I raided your chest of drawers. I hope you don't mind.' He pulled a little face. 'She had a little accident.'

'No problem.' Dora smiled at the little girl. 'Hello, Sophie,' she said. 'Now that you're up, would you like some eggs?'

She'd made toast, and now she cut a slice into triangles and spread on the scrambled egg.

Gannon translated for the child, speaking in a language that sounded familiar, and Sophie's eyes widened as he propped himself on a stool, held her on his knee and offered her the plate. She ate quickly with her fingers, scarcely pausing to chew, gathering up even the smallest crumbs.

'There's more,' Dora offered.

But Gannon shook his head. 'That's enough for now.' He pulled his plate towards him and began to eat awkwardly, with one hand.

'Here, you can't eat like that. Give her to me.'

He didn't argue, but when Dora bent to take her Sophie clung to him.

He spoke to her gently, his voice encouraging her, and Dora found herself subjected to a close scrutiny by the solemn-faced little girl. Then, as if satisfied with what she saw, Sophie raised her arms to her in a gesture of absolute trust.

'Oh, sweetheart, you're cold. I'll take her by the fire, Gannon.'

'Sure,' he said, but she hadn't waited for his permission. Sophie's feet were freezing, and Dora carried her to the armchair by the fire, curling up with her in her lap. For a moment Sophie stared at Dora's long fair hair. Then, bolder, she reached out and touched it.

'Hair,' Dora said.

Sophie repeated the word, smiled, then, still holding onto a long golden strand, closed her eyes and was immediately asleep. Dora, unable to move without disturbing the child, made the best of it, relaxing back against the chair, and as the heat of the fire began to make her drowsy, she closed her eyes.

When Gannon came looking for

them five minutes later, they were both fast asleep, wrapped in each other's arms. He stood over them for a moment, considering whether to carry Sophie back to bed. It seemed a pity to disturb her again, and maybe she would feel safer like this. And he could take the opportunity to have a few minutes' rest, knowing that Sophie would wake him if Dora moved.

He made up the fire, piling on logs and replacing the guard, before stretching out in the armchair opposite Dora and Sophie. Yet, despite an almost desperate weariness, he was reluctant to close his eyes, blot out a scene of such utter peacefulness.

The woman and child had fallen asleep sure in the knowledge that they were safe, that nothing would harm them. For a moment his mind drifted back over the last forty-eight hours, and he knew that the peace was temporary. At least for him and Sophie.

★   ★   ★

Dora woke feeling stiff and uncomfortable. Her head was at an awkward angle and her left arm was numb, and for a moment she couldn't work out where she was. Then she blinked as she saw the man stretched out in the chair opposite, his head thrown back against the cushions, his long, thin body relaxed in sleep, and it all came flooding back. The break-in. Sophie. Gannon.

Most of all she remembered Gannon, impossible, overbearing and arrogant, and her cheeks heated up at the way she had tried to stare him down in the bathroom. John Gannon was not a man to play chicken with.

And she remembered the telephone, upstairs in her bedroom. She'd curled up with Sophie in front of the fire because the child had been cold and she must have nodded off. Now it was too late. Or was it? Gannon was fast asleep. Food and warmth had done their work, relaxing him so that the exhaustion that shadowed his eyes had finally caught up with him.

Asleep he looked so much less threatening. With his head thrown back so that his long throat was exposed he seemed, on the contrary, to be almost vulnerable. At her mercy.

In repose, the hard planes of his face had lost the taut, hunted look of her midnight marauder. He didn't look like a marauder at all, she thought. More like an academic, or an artist.

A lock of dark hair had fallen across his forehead, softening the high ascetic forehead, the hollowed temples, and his watchful eyes, which by some trick of the light seemed to alternate between gold and agate, were lidded and fringed with thick, dark lashes.

His long straight nose, his firm mouth, the uncompromising chin all suggested a man of infinite strength and endurance. He was, she thought with a little inward flip somewhere in the region of her waist, strikingly beautiful.

He didn't look in the least bit dangerous, more like a man who could be anyone's brother or uncle. She looked down at the child curled up against her shoulder. Or loving father. But looks could be deceptive. And there was more than one kind of danger.

Sophie seemed absolutely dead to the world too. Heaven alone knew what the child had been through, but she was clearly under-nourished and suffering from exhaustion. Maybe she would be able to carry her up to bed without waking her.

But as she tried to ease forward those big dark eyes flew open and the little body tensed in her arms. Before she could cry out, Dora placed a finger to her lips with an almost silent 'Shh,' and she looked meaningfully towards Gannon. Sophie seemed to instantly understand that silence was necessary. Still tense, she turned to look at Gannon. Then, as she realised why Dora wanted her to be quiet, she too put her finger to her lips. Dora smiled approvingly, and as Sophie smiled back her thin face lit up.

So far, so good.

She managed to stand, still holding

the child, although her cramped muscles complained bitterly at their mistreatment as she stepped carefully over Gannon's outstretched legs. She tried hard not to look at him, sure that he would somehow feel her gaze on him and stir.

She crept silently towards the door, sure with every step that his low voice would break the silence to ask her where she was going. But she made it to the door without disturbing him, climbed the stairs, and then she was in the bedroom, her heart pounding like a kettledrum by the time she eased Sophie onto the bed.

She made another gesture for silence before groping beneath the bed for the telephone, wasting no time about punching in the one number she knew by heart. There was no time to waste calling directory enquiries, and she didn't have time to look up Sarah's number in the little book she carried with her. Even if Gannon hadn't taken her bag away.

It seemed to take for ever before the distant telephone began to ring, and when finally it was answered it wasn't her brother but his housekeeper. Well, it was still early.

'Can I speak to Fergus, please?' she whispered.

'I'm sorry, I can't hear you very well — the line isn't too good,' Mrs Harris said.

'Fergus,' she hissed desperately. 'Is he there?'

'I don't think he's down yet. Just one moment.' Dora heard the receiver being placed on the hall table and Mrs Harris's retreating footsteps across the hall. There was a long pause, in which Dora held her breath.

Then suddenly she heard the receiver lifted and Fergus's cool voice saying simply, 'Kavanagh.'

And she knew exactly what his reaction would be. He'd be patronising. Just the way he had been when she had first told him about her plans to drive an aid truck into eastern Europe

— certain that she'd be on the phone to him within a week begging for help. *And she remembered her silent avowal that she would chew glass first.*

Now here she was, with not one but three nightmare journeys into Grasnia with relief supplies safely behind her — three journeys when even if she had screamed at the top of her voice her well-connected brother could have done nothing to help her. She'd survived exhaustion, hostile soldiers, primitive conditions, the lack of clean water and decent food, the horrors of the refugee camps. The gunfire.

Now, when she was safe home, was she really going to rush to Fergus for help at the first small problem to confront her? He was a hundred miles away, for heaven's sake. What could he do? More importantly, what *would* he do? It didn't take a vast imagination to work that out. He'd call the Chief Constable — he was bound to know him — and demand an armed interven-tion unit be sent to the cottage to extricate his sister from some terrible hostage situation she had got herself into.

All right, no one could describe Gannon's eruption into her life with Sophie as something particularly desirable, but did she *really* need Fergus to come riding to her rescue?

She'd gone to Grasnia to give help, not take it. She'd been looking for a challenge. Yet when a full-blown one walked right up and broke in through her own front door all she could think of doing was yelling for help.

If Gannon was who he said he was, she was in no danger. If she'd been frightened she wouldn't have come creeping upstairs this morning, she'd have taken the opportunity to make a run for it. If she'd wanted the police, she could have called them herself.

Sophie was kneeling on the bed, her huge dark eyes solemn as she watched her, her head tilted a little to one side, as if waiting for Dora to decide.

'Hello? Hello? Is there anybody

there?' Fergus's voice was insistent in her ear. One word, that was all it would take to bring the forces of law and order rushing to her aid. But when he had mocked her plans she had told him that she was all grown up. Perhaps it was time she started demonstrating the fact. Her instincts told her that Gannon would not harm her. And adults had to trust their instincts, didn't they?

Gannon and Sophie were in some kind of trouble. Maybe she was being stupid, but she suddenly realised that she wanted to help them as much as any of the wretched refugees she had met in Grasnia.

'I'm terribly sorry, I have the wrong number,' she mumbled quickly, so that he shouldn't recognise her voice. And before she could change her mind, she disconnected the call and slotted the phone back into the charger, pushing it back out of sight beneath the bed. Then, raking her hair back from her face with her fingers, she smiled at

Sophie. 'Come on, sweetheart, I think you could do with a bath.'

* * *

Gannon woke slowly, coming out of a deep sleep in a series of waves, each one shallower than the last until he opened his eyes and was fully awake. He stretched, and although he was still aware of the pain in his side it was less raw. Maybe he hadn't done as much damage as he thought. Or maybe he just felt so much better with food inside him and the first uninterrupted sleep he'd had in days that he didn't notice it as much.

But it was colder, the fire was little more than embers, and he shivered in the early-morning air. What he needed was some hot coffee, then he would be fit to face the raft of problems that were piling up.

But as he straightened, rubbing his hands over his face to wake himself more fully, he realised that he would have to put coffee and eggs on hold, because one problem wouldn't wait. The chair on the other side of the hearth was empty. Sophie and Dora were gone.

5

Gannon was on his feet and halfway to the back door when he heard laughter. He stopped, completely taken aback by such an unexpected sound. Then there was a shriek, and he spun round and raced for the stairs.

Dora, kneeling beside the bath and swooshing water through her hands at Sophie, turned as he burst into the bathroom. 'Hi,' she said, smiling up at him. She was wearing a huge baggy T-shirt in duck-egg blue and a pair of black leggings that clung to her like a second skin. Her hair was tied back with a band and she was bereft of make-up. There was nothing calculated about the way she looked. But she looked stunning. 'We're having fun,' she said. 'Want to play?'

He swallowed, rooted to the spot. Play? Had she any idea what she was saying? 'I wondered where you were,' he said, stiffly.

'Where would we be? But it seemed a pity to disturb you,' she said with a smile, her wide mouth disturbing him altogether too much. 'You looked so peaceful.' *Really? He wasn't feeling that way now.* 'And I thought Sophie would enjoy a bath.'

'You would appear to be right.'

'Mmm.' She moved along to make space for him, and patted the side of the bath invitingly. 'I warn you, Sophie likes to splash.'

'Does she?' He knelt beside her, but he wasn't looking at Sophie. Dora had showered, her hair was still damp, and she smelled deliciously of soap and shampoo and he couldn't take his eyes off her. For a moment, as they stared at one another, he felt as if he'd known her all his life. Then Sophie, tired of being ignored, showered him with a well-aimed jet of water and he turned on her, splashing her back, making her squeal with laughter until she was begging him to stop.

As he turned away to pull a towel from the shelf he realised that Dora was still staring at him, her concentration so intent that there was a tiny furrow between her brows. 'Dora?'

For a heart-stopping moment she continued to look at him. Then she turned quickly away and, grabbing a towel, bent over the bath to scoop Sophie out. 'Why don't you go and make a start on breakfast, Gannon?' she said abruptly. 'While I look for something a bit more suitable for Sophie to wear.'

'Anything special?' She shook her head, but didn't look back at him. 'Right.'

'And perhaps you could relight the fire. It's not very warm this morning. I don't want her to get cold.'

'Leave it with me.'

'And, John.' He paused in the doorway, and this time he was the one determined not to look round. 'I'll do whatever I can to help.'

Despite himself, he glanced back at her. She was standing, feet slightly parted, Sophie in her arms, and the early-morning light was making a halo out of the wisps of hair that had escaped the band. In that moment he knew exactly why Richard had fallen for her, why in an age where most people just lived together he had married her, so that she would always be his. In Richard's place he would have done exactly the same. He nodded, and without another word headed back downstairs.

Once he had disappeared from sight, Dora let out a long-held breath. She was what the media termed a 'Sloane', one of the 'girls in pearls' who divided their time between Henley and Ascot and the Hurlingham Club. She was used to being stared at, but when John Gannon looked at her something seemed to heat up inside her, some secret place inside her that she hadn't known existed. And then the heat began to spread.

Sophie put her thin arms about her neck, hugging her tightly, and Dora turned to smile at the child, kiss her thin cheek. 'Come on, darling. Let's find you something to wear.'

Dora sorted through her drawers and found nothing that was of any real use to Sophie. She was just so tiny, so terribly thin, that Dora's baggy T-shirts swamped her. Was that the reason Gannon had snatched her? Because she had been cruelly neglected?

Whatever the reason, Sophie couldn't tell her. She bundled her up as best she could to keep her warm, and gave her a hug before carrying her downstairs. 'This child needs clothes, Gannon,' she said briskly.

He glanced up from the cooker. 'She looks fine to me.'

'Don't be silly. She's got no under-wear for a start.'

'I don't suppose it bothers her.'

'I don't suppose it does, much. But what about shoes? I've tried putting my socks on her but they just fall off, and her feet are cold.'

He shifted uncomfortably. 'The fire will soon get going.'

'That's a rather temporary solution. Or are you planning to stay here until she grows into my things?'

It was a tempting thought. 'No. Under the circumstances, the sooner we go the better.'

'What circumstances?'

That he had snatched his daughter from a refugee camp without permission. That the British and French police would soon be looking for him, if they weren't already. That he was in grave danger of making a fool of himself over a friend's wife.

All of them were pressing reasons for leaving the cottage, but none of them would make a very graceful exit line, would they?

Dora grew tired of waiting for an answer. 'Where will you go, Gannon? And what about Sophie? You can't just walk out of the door with her. She's just a baby. She needs warmth, shelter. She needs to be looked after.'

He had no argument with that, but escape had been the only thing on his mind — getting the child to safety. Once they were at the cottage he'd known they would be able to rest, recuperate, and he would have time to think. He hadn't counted on company. The only alternative was his own flat in London, but that was the first place the authorities would look. He began to crack eggs into a pan. 'I'm open to suggestions.'

'Are you?' Dora wasn't so sure, but she tried one for size. 'Well, why don't we deal with one problem at a time? Before you can take her anywhere Sophie has to have some clothes. So, I'll go into town and buy her some.' She saw him struggle with this. 'Or you could go and I'll stay with Sophie,' she offered.

He stared at her, trying desperately to get inside her head, work out what was making her tick, but she had put down the shutters and her dark grey eyes were like mirrors.

'Can I trust you?'

'Trust me to do what? Buy clothes? Or keep your presence here a secret?' Dora looked around. 'I don't see anyone else. I guess you'll have to.' She placed Sophie on a stool. 'Right, young lady. How do you fancy a bowl of cornflakes?' She rattled the box, and Sophie grinned back at her.

⋆ ⋆ ⋆

As soon as Sophie had been fed Dora went to find a tape measure to run over her. And she drew outlines around the child's feet, which made her laugh as the pencil tickled.

'Where are you going to shop?' he asked, as she prepared to leave.

'Nowhere without my car keys.' She was checking the contents of her bag. 'I seem to have mislaid them.'

He fished them out of his pocket and handed them to her. 'I suppose you'll need this, too,' he said, looking at her wallet, with its stack of credit cards.

'I suppose I will.' He briefly considered keeping the cash, but couldn't bring himself to remove it in the face of the slightly old-fashioned look she was giving him. He just pushed it into her hand. 'I'll pop into Maybridge,' she said, finally answering his question. 'It's the nearest place of any size.'

'Keep a note of what you spend,' he said, somewhat unnecessarily he realised, in view of her propensity to hoard receipts. 'I'll repay you as soon as I can get to a bank.'

'Please don't feel you have to hold one up to repay me. Buying Sophie a few clothes won't break me.'

He remembered the extravagant receipts for her own wardrobe. 'Or Richard?'

Suddenly she wasn't as bold, he noticed, as her gaze slid away, refusing the direct challenge. 'I'm sure he'd do the same if he were here,' she muttered. 'I'll be as quick as I can.'

He followed her out to the far end of

the barn, now used to garage Richard's bruising great four-wheel drive. Poppy's bright little sports car stood next to it. Her own dark green Mini seemed very tame alongside them, but she wasn't interested in turning heads.

'You've got a lot of horsepower for two people,' Gannon said as he pulled open the door so that she could drive out.

'This is just my shopping trolley.' Dora strapped herself into her seat before looking up at him. 'But if you should be thinking about legging it before I get back, I should warn you now; Richard immobilised those two before he left.'

Gannon grinned. 'Doesn't he trust you with his prized wheels?'

Dora widened her mouth in a humourless smile. 'Maybe Richard knows his friends better than they know him.' She leaned forward and started the engine. 'When I get back, Gannon, you'd better be prepared to tell me what's going on.' She flipped open a pair of sunglasses she kept on the dashboard and slipped them on. 'Who knows? If I think you're a deserving case I might come up with some bright ideas to help.'

She didn't give him time to return some smart answer, but backed neatly out, swung around in the yard and headed for the lane.

Gannon watched her drive away, wondering if he was making a really big mistake. On balance, he thought not. But you could never be sure. There was something about her that he couldn't put his finger on. And it bothered him. Or perhaps it was just that *she* bothered him.

He turned quickly and re-entered the house, locking the door behind him. Then, calling to Sophie to follow him, he went upstairs. He helped her up onto Dora's bed and told her to stay there, quietly, while he showered and changed. He spoke to her first in her own language and then in English. The sooner she became fluent the better.

'Is Dora coming back?' Sophie asked.

Gannon answered her, repeating the words slowly for her in English, 'I hope so, sweetheart. Snuggle down there and keep warm. I won't be long.'

He showered, shaved and then sorted through Richard's wardrobe. He had never been as thickly built as Richard, and he'd lost a hell of a lot of weight in the last few months, but he cinched in a belt and looked presentable enough in a pair of casual trousers, a soft shirt and a jacket. But he was in no hurry to leave the room. He felt less constrained about looking around with Dora out of the house, and he wandered around the bedroom, checking the slightly different view from the window to see if anyone was about. But the area alongside the river was deserted. Not a fisherman in sight.

He glanced into the *en suite* bathroom, furnished in much the same style as the guest bathroom, the twin basins provided with expensive his and hers toiletries. Another door led into a beautifully fitted dressing room. He opened the walk-in closet and whistled softly at the array of expensive clothes.

The receipts in Dora's handbag had clearly been just the tip of the iceberg, he realised, as his eyes swept over the rainbow colours of exquisite evening gowns and elegant daywear. Hardly the everyday wardrobe of a woman who lived quietly in the country — a woman who wore leggings and a sloppy T-shirt to visit the local shops and who tied her hair back with an elastic band, he thought. It all seemed just a little sophisticated for Dora.

And yet, right at the back of the closet, not quite covered by white sheeting, was indisputable proof that she had told him the truth. He lifted the cover to reveal a wedding gown in heavy ivory silk with a matching hooded cloak in velvet. Very simple, very sophisticated. Absolutely perfect for a Christmas wedding. He dropped the cover and spun round, scarcely feeling the protest from his ribs at the sudden movement. Until that moment, he realised, he hadn't actually believed that Richard and Dora were married. Hadn't wanted to believe it.

What an idiot! Gannon crossed to the window and stared out at the familiar view. He just didn't understand. What on earth had gone wrong between them? Obviously something serious. Why else would Dora have moved into the guest bedroom when all her beautiful clothes were stored in the dressing room?

He returned to Sophie. He had problems enough of his own, without worrying about Richard and Dora, yet he needed to make some sense of what was going on. He glanced at the small pine wardrobe and without a twinge of conscience opened the door, searching for something that would explain why she had moved out of the main bedroom.

He was staring at the contents of the wardrobe, his forehead puckered in a deep frown as he tried to work out what was bothering him, when he heard a long, low beep. Sophie giggled, and the sound was repeated. He half turned. The child was playing with something half hidden by the folds of the bedcover. Had Dora found the child a toy of some kind?

Then, as he took a step towards her, it began to ring. Sophie let out a cry of surprise, looking at him with such a comical 'I-didn't-do-it' look that he almost laughed. Almost.

'It's all right, sweetheart,' he said, with a reassurance he was far from feeling as the ringing continued. 'It's just a telephone.' *Just a telephone.* He'd heard himself saying the words and could scarcely believe it. He picked it up and held it, uncertain whether to answer it or let it ring. In the event the decision was made for him when the caller gave up.

Dear God, but she was a cool customer. She could have called half the county while he had been down-stairs sleeping in front of the fire. She probably had. Then she had told him that she wanted to help, called him John in that soft, seductive voice of hers, and calmly suggested that she drive into town to buy clothes for Sophie. She had made it all sound so reasonable that he'd given her back her car keys without a qualm. Well, without much of one. And, because she'd need some cash, he'd handed back her wallet for good measure.

Cool! Ice cream wouldn't melt in her mouth. Despite himself, he was impressed.

So, who had she called? Richard? Surely she would have called him first? If she had it would account for the fact that this morning she seemed so much less tense, so much more willing to help.

He'd almost convinced himself that must be the case when he heard the sound of a car making its way slowly up the lane.

It was too soon for Dora to return, unless she'd forgotten something, and he crossed swiftly to the window. No, it wasn't Dora. It was a police patrol car. He'd teased Dora that her young constable would make some excuse to return, but he hadn't expected it to be at ten o'clock in the morning.

Then from his vantage point he saw another vehicle, a big police transit van, following it. He stepped back, and, sparing just enough breath for one muttered curse, swept Sophie up, heading down the stairs before his escape was cut off. Her blanket, dry now, was folded up on the sofa. He flung down the telephone and grabbed it.

The lane led naturally around to the rear of the cottage, and to use what had originally been the front door it was necessary to walk around the path. Gannon took the few moments of grace given him to slip out that way, and, crouching low behind the hedge, ignoring the breath-snatching pain scything through his ribs, he headed for the shelter of a small copse.

He paused there to gather his breath

and wipe away the cold sweat standing out on his forehead. Sophie made no sound. She had been through situations like this too many times to cry out. But she clung to him, her face buried in the collar of his jacket, and she was rigid with fear.

One of the men looked in the direction of the copse and Gannon edged slowly back, deeper into cover. And with every step he silently cursed the girl who had betrayed them in such a calculated manner. Had she thought he would hold her hostage against his own safety if the police arrived mob-handed while she was there? Was that what she had told them?

He slumped against a tree. He could scarcely blame her. But she had told him that she would do what she could to help him. She'd looked at him with those beautiful eyes, said his name, and with every cell in his body panting he had wanted to believe her. Oh, how he'd wanted to believe her.

He watched the police circle the

cottage. What had she done? Told them she would call them when she was clear of the cottage? Tell them when it was safe to move in . . .

* * *

The problem with shopping for little girls, Dora discovered as she browsed through the mouthwatering selection of clothes in the comfortable anonymity of a chainstore, was not deciding what to buy but knowing when to stop. There was just so much to choose from, each dress, each frilly pair of socks, each cute pair of dungarees simply crying out 'buy me'. But for the moment function was more important than frills. And, since little girls seemed to prefer jeans, sweatshirts, slouch socks and trainers to lace and smocking, she confined herself to those, although indulged herself by choosing the prettiest underpinnings she could find.

She chose a bright, padded weather-proof coat to top it all, and handed it to the cashier. Then she spotted a rag doll. It wasn't very big but it had a mop of black wool hair and reminded her so much of Sophie that she couldn't resist it. She paid with a credit card and then headed for the bank.

She didn't even wonder at the casual manner in which she had written a cheque for five hundred pounds as she waited while the clerk checked her account. In for a penny.

Not that Gannon had asked her to get money for him, but it seemed an even bet that he would need some. Of course, she wasn't planning on simply handing it over, no questions asked.

The money would stay tucked safely out of his reach until he had told her exactly what was going on. Where would be safe? Not her handbag, that was for sure. The bra was the classic hiding place. She recollected any number of films where she had seen sexy ladies push loot into a generous cleavage. The trouble was Gannon had probably seen them too. She started out of her reverie as she realised that the bank clerk was regarding her impatiently, clearly awaiting some response.

'Sorry,' she said, 'did you say something?'

'How would you like the money, Miss Kavanagh?'

'Oh. Tens and twenties, please. No, wait, tens would be better. Just tens.'

Dora watched as the woman counted out the money and pushed it towards her. It made quite a pile. If she stashed it in her bra Gannon couldn't fail to spot the sudden increase in her forward projection, and if he needed the cash, she didn't think he would hesitate to investigate. Suppressing a giggle, she thanked the clerk and stuffed the notes in her bag. She'd worry about what she'd do with the money when she got back to the car.

She walked back through the shopping centre, stopping at the bakers for some fresh bread and doughnuts. And then, as she passed the big newsagents and bookshop, she stopped and went inside. The foreign dictionaries and phrasebooks were stacked with the guidebooks and maps, and she quickly found what she was looking for, taking it to the desk and putting it on the corner of the counter next to a pile of local newspapers while she delved in her bag for her wallet.

Then, as she retrieved the book, she caught sight of the banner headline. STOLEN PLANE IN EMERGENCY LANDING IN FIELD.

For a moment she remained frozen to the spot, totally oblivious to the fact that the cashier was holding out her hand for her purchase.

It couldn't be Gannon. Really. No. The whole idea was too melodramatic for words.

Then a little shoosh of air exploded between her teeth. Last night had been the very stuff of melodrama. Nothing had been missing.

Menacing thunder, lightning to illuminate the scene as a desperate man burdened by a small child crossed rain-soaked fields in search of shelter. Then his arrival at a cottage where a young woman, alone and defenceless, lay sleeping.

It wasn't just melodramatic, it was pure Gothic. All it lacked was a corny score and Hammer Horror titles rolling over the opening action.

Except the whole thing was quite ridiculous. Gannon couldn't possibly have stolen a plane. She picked up a copy of the newspaper. Why would he?

She glanced at the phrasebook in her hand and the answer stared right back at her. She'd been to the refugee camps, met and spoken to children just like Sophie. She wasn't his daughter. She was a refugee. But why would a man steal a plane to smuggle a child out of a refugee camp?

The answer was plain enough. She had been there, she had held the children and cried for them, even for a few desperate days pleaded with the aid agency to let her adopt one of them. But what good would that do? How could you choose which child to help? The aid workers had seen it all before, and they had very gently talked her out of it, reassuring her that what she was doing would help *all* the children.

But Gannon hadn't allowed himself to be diverted. He had acted. But to steal a plane . . .

She continued to stare at the paper, hoping against hope that she was wrong. Gannon genuinely cared for Sophie. She had seen it in the way he looked at the child, heard it in his voice when he spoke to her so very gently. But if the police caught up with him they would surely send Sophie back. They wouldn't have a choice.

'Next,' the woman behind the till said pointedly, and Dora started out of her reverie.

'Sorry, I was dreaming,' she apologised.

'Do you want the paper?'

Did she? Ignorance is bliss, she reminded herself. Except it wasn't. For the last few hours she had been

142

operating on the foolish notion that helping Gannon was the right thing to do. Deep down, where the unexplained certainties had taken hold, she was quite sure that it was. But it wouldn't hurt to make quite, *quite* sure that he wasn't some dangerous criminal on the run from every police force this side of the Urals.

'Yes. Thank you.' She paid, and then settled herself in a nearby café, ordered coffee she didn't want and with a miserable, sinking feeling, spread out the paper and began to read.

Despite the banner headline, and the harshly lit photograph of a small, single-engined plane that seemed to be listing slightly to one side, the report contained just the barest facts.

Police are hunting for the pilot of a single-engine Cessna who made an emergency landing at Marsh Farm last night. The aircraft, which is believed to have been stolen from a private field outside Paris, was slightly damaged during the landing. By the time the emergency services arrived the pilot had disappeared, and is thought to have escaped on foot. Local police are appealing to anyone who picked up a hitchhiker late last night in the vicinity of Marsh Farm to get in touch.

The rest was simply speculation about the identity of the pilot. She didn't read it because she knew his identity.

A plane. He'd stolen a plane, for heaven's sake. What kind of man was capable of stealing a plane? The answer was inescapable. A desperate man. A desperate man on the run with a little girl.

Sophie. Dora didn't bother to drink the coffee. She threw down some coins, grabbed her bags and ran.

* * *

Gannon watched the police circling the cottage, poking about the outbuildings, the woodstore. He could hear them banging on the back door, and he could see the two officers who had taken up position by the front door in case he made a break for it. Another minute and he would have been trapped.

Across the field, he heard the splintering crack as the door was broken in. Sophie whimpered and shivered against him, and he tightened his hold, murmured soft, reassuring words, telling her that she was safe, that he wouldn't leave her. That he would *never* leave her. But in his head he cursed his own folly for having trusted Dora. How could he have been so stupid?

Because she had looked at him with limpid grey eyes and told him that she wanted to help. And like an idiot he had believed her.

★   ★   ★

Dora sped back to the cottage, skidding to a halt just inches from a police car parked across the yard. The cottage door, splintered and broken where the lock had been smashed, stood wide open.

Her stomach turned over. Gannon had been arrested; Sophie had been taken away. Were they going to arrest her as an accomplice? She groaned. If Fergus had to bail her out of this mess she would never hear the last of it.

Maybe she didn't deserve to, a small but insistent inner voice prompted. About to be arrested for harbouring a wanted man, she was scarcely in a position to expect anything but scorn from her brother. She could scarcely plead ignorance — the newspaper, with its banner headline, lay on the back seat of the Mini. But had she rushed to the nearest police station with her information? Oh, no. She'd gone to the bank and cashed a cheque, bought clothes for Sophie . . .

For heaven's sake! What happened to

her didn't matter. It was Sophie's plight that was fuelling her. And if Gannon had been locked up, who was there left to look after her? Fight for her?

Dora gripped the steering wheel. Whatever happened, she wouldn't let that child be taken back. Not if she had to take on the whole British establishment, the entire bureaucracy of Europe single-handed to keep her safe. But she wouldn't be able to help anyone if she was locked up.

She was shaking, but it had nothing to do with the close call with the patrol car. It was pure determination. She braced herself for the fight as the policemen headed towards her, not waiting for them but clambering out of the Mini and rushing across to the shattered door. There was no sign of a struggle; everything was just as she left it. She spun around.

'What's happened?' she demanded indignantly. *What? These were police-men, for heaven's sake. Was she going to lie to them?* She thought of the

147

horrors of the refugee camp, thought of Sophie. Of course she was going to lie. 'Who did this?' Her voice was shaking, but shaking was fine. Shaking was a natural reaction.

'I'm sorry, miss. We had information that a fugitive might be taking shelter here.'

'A fugitive?' she repeated, then frowned. It wasn't difficult. 'Are you telling me that *you* did this?'

The older officer spoke. 'I'm Sergeant Willis, miss. This is Constable Martin.'

'We met last night.'

'Yes, well, perhaps we could all go inside? We have one or two questions to ask you; it won't take long. Pete, bring the young lady's shopping, will you? I expect she'd like a cup of tea, too.'

'That isn't necessary,' Dora snapped. 'Who's going to pay for all this damage?' The sergeant was not intimidated, but indicated the back door, and having made her point, Dora walked stiffly into the living room, all outraged innocence, before turning to face him. 'I'd like some kind of explanation,' she said.

'The thing is, miss, that as part of our investigation into another incident we've been following up all last night's unexplained alarms.'

'So?'

'We've discovered from Mr Marriott's security company that he and Mrs Marriott are in the United States. And the lady who cleans the cottage for Mrs Marriott was told that it would be empty for six weeks. So, although last night when Constable Martin called you allowed him to think you were Mrs Marriott, that is clearly not the case.' He was being incredibly polite, but Dora did not doubt that he wanted some answers. 'So perhaps, miss, you could begin by explaining who you are and how you happen to have keys to this cottage?'

6

Dora stared at the man.

'You mean all this . . . ' she waved imperiously in the direction of the smashed door ' . . . is because last night I didn't waste Constable Martin's time correcting his mistaken impression that I was my sister?'

'Your sister?'

She turned to Pete Martin. The young man had done his job well, and she didn't want to get him into trouble, but if it came to him or Sophie there was no contest. Still, it wouldn't hurt to be apologetic. Very apologetic. 'Perhaps I should have explained,' she conceded, 'but it was so late . . . and you were so busy . . . ' she added, conveniently forgetting his offer to come in and look around. 'I'm Poppy's sister. Dora Kavanagh.' She extended her hand to the younger man, and after a moment's hesitation he took it. 'I'm so glad to have the chance to thank you for checking up on me last night. It's really very reassuring to know how vigilant you are.' She gestured towards the door. 'I suppose I might have been part of some gang using my sister's cottage as a hide-out — '

'Or possibly being held against your will by a desperate man. You've seen the paper,' he said, nodding to the local newspaper. 'When we couldn't get through on the telephone, and then saw that it had been disconnected — '

'Oh, no! You didn't think . . . ' Her fingers flew to her mouth. 'How embarrassing.' The policeman waited. 'It's been playing up,' she said, improvising like mad. 'I took the cover off to see if it was a loose connection . . . ' She gave an embarrassed little shrug. 'I'd better give BT a ring and get a professional to sort it out.'

'That would be a good idea. You're house-sitting, Miss Kavanagh?' the sergeant enquired.

'Not house-sitting exactly. I'm just staying for a few days. London was getting to be a bit of a strain, and Poppy gave me a set of keys before she left for the States, in case I wanted a bolthole.'

She'd breezed in on a cloud of Joy on her way to the airport. 'I can't stop, Richard is downstairs with a stopwatch, but I've had Fergus on the phone, worried to death about you.'

'Worried to death that I missed Henley, Ascot and Wimbledon, all in the same summer. What that man needs is a wife; that would give him something to *really* worry him.'

'I know. Still . . . ' The phone had begun to ring, interrupting her flow, and Poppy had looked at it with more than a touch of irritation. 'Ignore it, it'll be Richard telling me to get a move on.' But, evidently deciding that her husband wouldn't be ignored for long, she'd produced a set of keys. 'Why don't you go down to the cottage for a week or two while Richard and I are in the States? Not a soul will know you're there, and you'll have time to think about what you're going to do next in perfect peace.' She'd grinned. 'Did I mention that Fergus is coming to London, determined to carry you back to Marlowe Court so that he can keep an eye on you?'

Dora looked at the two policemen as she recalled her sister's words. *Peace!* She'd have had more peace on the hard shoulder of the M25. 'Well, don't let me keep you gentlemen. I imagine you're keen to get on with more important things.'

They didn't move. 'I suppose you can *prove* that you're Mrs Marriott's sister?'

She stared at the sergeant. 'I suppose I can, if it's quite necessary.' He did not respond, and she gave a little gasp. 'You don't *still* think I might be hiding this man?'

'No, no . . . ' Pete began. The older man didn't look so certain.

'It doesn't say much about him in the local paper. Is he dangerous?' She put on a good show of nervousness. It wasn't difficult. She wasn't acting.

'We don't know who he is, Miss Kavanagh. But it's possible he's a smuggler.' He took the bright bags off the sofa and glanced inside them. 'You've been busy yourself. You look as if you've been buying up the store. Who's the lucky child?' he asked.

'My niece,' she said, saying the first thing that came into her head.

'Your niece? I didn't think Mr and Mrs Marriott had any children.'

He'd been doing his homework. Or someone had. 'They haven't. Actually, it's my sister's niece, Laurie. She lives on the other side of the village. Her mother is Sarah Shelton. Her husband owns a number of companies . . . '

'I *know* who you are,' the constable broke in excitedly. 'You're that woman that's been in all the newspapers. The society lady who's been helping the refugees.'

And suddenly the older policeman's face broke into a broad smile. 'Of course. I thought I'd seen you some-where before.'

She pulled a face. 'Don't tell me. You thought it was on your 'most wanted' list. No wonder you were so suspicious.'

He laughed, but with a slight awkwardness that suggested she wasn't that far from the truth. 'My wife was in tears when you were on the television . . . I don't suppose you'd sign something for her?'

'I'd be happy to.' She cast around, looking for something suitable, anxious for the men to be gone. A few moments later she turned to hand the officer a sheet of her sister's notepaper with her signature on it, and realised that Pete was staring at something. For a moment her heart stopped beating. What? What had he seen?

But it was just the phrasebook she had bought. She'd put it in with the clothes, rather than take another bag, and it had slipped out when the constable had put them down on the sofa.

'You're even learning the language,' he said, in awe.

She managed a laugh. She actually managed a laugh. 'Not exactly. I just thought that it would be useful to learn a few helpful phrases for my next trip.'

* * *

Dora closed the back door behind the two policemen and leaned weakly against it. She had begun to think they would never go.

It was Pete's radio which finally, thankfully, had interrupted the flow. 'We're wanted back at base, Sarge,' he'd said, heading for the door.

'I'll be right out.' The sergeant had immediately become businesslike. 'You'll need to get someone to fix the door, Miss Kavanagh.'

'Don't worry, I have someone I can call.'

'Yes, well, if your sister wants to make a claim, she can pick up a form from the station.'

'I shouldn't think so. You were just doing your job.'

'To be honest, we were concerned about your safety. We thought he must have stolen your car. You might have been lying in here hurt, or worse.'

'Well, as you see, I'm perfectly safe.' *But where were Gannon and Sophie?*

'If you do see anything suspicious you will give us a call, Miss Kavanagh, won't you?'

'Surely your man will be miles away by now?'

'Possibly. But it wouldn't be wise to take any risks.'

'I won't.' Her subconscious had responded with a hoot of hollow laughter. 'If I do see anything, I'll call 999 without delay.'

'If it's a real emergency don't hesitate, but this is the number of the local police station.' He'd produced a card and written his name on the back. 'And call BT and get the phone fixed. Or I'll call them if you like.' He'd nodded at the mobile phone, lying on the sofa. 'Those things can let you down at the vital moment.'

Tell me about it. She'd snatched the phone up and switched it on. There'd been a satisfactory beep. 'It's fine,' she'd said. 'I'll do it straight away.'

'Good. Any other queries, just ring me at the station. I'll come straight over.' He'd handed her the card.

'That's kind of you.'

She'd seen them to the car and, although a few heavy drops of rain had been beginning to fall, watched while Pete reversed and drove with pointed care around the Mini. She'd watched until the car had manoeuvred the drive and was out in the lane, gathering speed towards the village. Only then had she gone back inside the cottage, her legs like weak jelly as she closed the door.

Finally she gathered the strength to move. 'Gannon!' she shouted. 'They've gone.' Her voice seemed to echo through the empty house. She ran up the stairs. 'Gannon!' She flung open doors. 'I don't know where the devil you're hiding, but you can come out now.' Nothing. Silence.

She walked through the rooms that had been so recently searched by two very thorough policemen, yet she still somehow expected him to pop out from under the bed. 'Gannon!'

She went into the bathroom he had used and spotted the razor lying on the shelf. That wasn't very clever. But then she hadn't been prepared for a police search.

She looked down at the mobile phone she was still carrying about with her. She'd taken it from the policeman without thinking. He'd picked it up off the sofa and handed it to her, and she suddenly realised what that meant.

Gannon wasn't answering because he wasn't in the cottage. He'd found the telephone and thought she had betrayed him. No wonder the police hadn't caught him.

'Oh, John!' she cried despairingly. And then, as the rain began to spatter more insistently at the window, she raced down the stairs. She had to find him. Find little Sophie. Gannon was undoubtedly capable of looking after himself, but Sophie shouldn't be out in this weather with a cough. She'd get pneumonia. Maybe die. And it would be her fault. She grabbed Poppy's jacket from the back of the door and stepped out into the rain. Which way would they have gone?

If he'd thought the police were coming he'd stay off the lane, keep clear of the road nearest to the cottage. She skirted the barn and stared about her. The copse was the first shelter across the field, and there was a stile set into the fence further along, where an ancient footpath led to the village.

He'd have to go that way if he was going to get transport. And for a man who was capable of stealing a plane, taking a car was unlikely to prove very difficult. But he was in enough trouble already. Not that she cared about what happened to him, she told herself. All she was concerned about was Sophie.

She doubled back to the cottage, grabbed her handbag and the clothes she'd bought for Sophie, and threw them onto the back seat of the Mini. Then she executed a tight circle and headed down the lane.

★   ★   ★

Gannon, his collar turned up against the sudden squall, Sophie tucked beneath his jacket, was taking his time. Not that he had much choice. The run across the field had taken its toll of his strength. Besides, the last thing he wanted to do was blunder into some woman walking her dog in the woods and scare her half to death.

He couldn't believe he'd been such a fool. He should have taken her car and her money last night and got away while he could. He stopped and leaned against a tree, letting it take his weight and Sophie's for a moment while he regained his breath. He grunted. Who the devil was he kidding? Last night he wouldn't have got a mile before falling asleep at the wheel. He'd had no choice but to stay at the cottage.

'Dora,' the child whimpered. 'I want Dora.'

He stroked her head, sympathising with her. For a while back there he'd wanted her himself, but a wise man stuck to one impossible dream at a time.

★　★　★

Dora drove slowly along the lane, peering through wipers struggling with the downpour sluicing down the windscreen, trying to remember where the footpath crossed the road. Then she spotted the neat little green and white sign, pointing hopefully towards the overgrown thicket. She pulled over onto the verge and stopped.

It was possible that she'd missed him, she had no way of knowing how long ago he'd left the cottage, but the path wound tortuously through the woods.

She'd walked it one Sunday back in the winter, when she'd come down to have lunch with Poppy, and unless Gannon knew it well he would have been crazy to stray out of sight of the path. Of course, if he saw her car he might think it was some kind of trap and take the chance.

She moved the car further up the lane and pulled up in the shelter of an ancient beech tree. But that wouldn't do either. If he thought she'd betrayed him he wasn't going to come anywhere near her.

She climbed out, locked the car and, pulling the coat up around her ears, ran back to the footpath. There was no sign of him. There was no sign of anyone. Well, only a fool, or a man on the run, would choose to walk a muddy footpath in this awful driving rain. But if he wasn't going to come to her, she would have to go to him.

She was a hundred yards or so into the wood before she started to call his name softly.

'Gannon. It's Dora.' The woods seemed unusually silent. He was there somewhere.

She walked on a little way. 'Gannon,' she called. 'The police have gone.' Still there was nothing. 'I didn't call them. I didn't call anybody. I want to help.'

Dora was beginning to feel distinctly jumpy. She was sure she was being watched. At first she had thought it was Gannon, being cautious. Well, she could understand that.

Suddenly it occurred to her that it might not be Gannon. It might not have been him in the plane. She had no proof. There might really be some desperate man hiding from the police, capable of doing anything to get away. And then she sensed someone behind her.

She spun round and let out a little squeal of fright as she saw a figure standing on the path. It wasn't Gannon. 'Sophie!' It was Sophie, her tiny figure swathed in a man's jacket, her bare feet muddied, but as she moved forward to sweep the child up, carry her to warmth and safety, she was grabbed from behind, a man's hand over her mouth, another thrown about her, pinning her arms so that she couldn't move.

'Don't make a sound, Dora,' Gannon murmured, close to her ear. She couldn't have if she tried. She could have struggled, and she knew she could have hurt him, perhaps won her freedom. But she didn't. She understood his caution. He was holding her firmly, but he wasn't hurting her, and she had no wish to hurt him, no wish to frighten Sophie. So she remained perfectly still. For seemingly endless moments they remained there, a frozen tableau in the pouring rain. Then he gradually eased his hand away from her mouth. 'What do you want?' he demanded.

'Nothing,' she said carefully. 'All I want is for Sophie to be safe. My car is parked in the lane. There are clothes for her and there's five hundred pounds in my pocket, with the keys.' He said nothing. 'I know you found the mobile, Gannon, and I don't blame you for thinking that I called the police. But I didn't. I didn't call anyone.'

'Why not?' His voice was deeply suspicious, but his grip had loosened and she turned to face him, leaning back a little to look up into his face. His dark hair was clinging wetly to skin that had suddenly gone the colour of putty, he was soaked through, his shirt and trousers sticking to him, and he looked gaunt with pain. He should be in bed, not driving about with a small child in tow.

'Because I'm crazy. You're all over the front page of the local paper — at least, I assume it was you. The stolen plane?'

He pulled a face. 'Not stolen. Borrowed from a friend.'

'Like you were going to borrow the cottage? Without asking.'

'I'll have it repaired, return it, for heaven's sake, as soon as I can get things sorted out so that Sophie can stay here. Henri will understand.'

'Like Richard? You have a lot of understanding friends, Gannon.'

'I'd do the same for them. They know that.'

'Not from the inside of jail . . . ' She half turned as she heard the chink of a dog's collar, but Gannon stopped her. He half bent to pick up Sophie, but as he caught his breath Dora grabbed her instead. Then she saw the dog, a small liver and white springer spaniel bounding ahead of her mistress. It was Bonnie. And her mistress was Poppy's daily. What had she said about fools? 'It's Mrs Fuller. She mustn't see me, Gannon. She'll recognise me.' She hoisted Sophie up beneath her coat and turned to run, but Gannon caught her by the waist, swinging her round. And as the dog bounded up to them, jumping up at Dora's legs, he clasped her face between his hands and kissed her.

She gave a little gasp, and for a moment tried to draw back, but his arm tightened around her and his mouth came down hard on hers.

Gannon had had only one thought when he grabbed her, when he kissed her. To hide her identity, to protect her from the danger he had so thoughtlessly dragged her into. But by the time the dog's owner had called her to heel and hurried on, her expression tight with disapproval, he had forgotten all about his sensible, legitimate reason for kissing Dora. He was simply lost in the heady pleasure of his mouth moving over hers, the sweet scent of her skin, the warmth spreading through his veins, defying the soaking chill of the rain and heating him from the inside out.

It was Sophie's wriggling that finally parted them, and as Dora stepped back, a little flushed, suddenly and stupidly shy, the child whispered something to Gannon. He hushed her. 'Don't ask,' he warned, when Dora raised her brows.

'Why? What did she say?' He refused to meet her eyes, and she saw that colour had darkened his cheeks, too.

Something about them kissing, then. She laughed, but didn't press it. 'Come on. Let's get out of this rain.'

Gannon stared down into her face. She was laughing. Not angry. Not offended that what should have been nothing but a pretence, a way to hide her face, had escalated into the real thing. No. Well, it hadn't escaped his notice that once she had got used to the idea Dora had kissed him back with considerable enthusiasm.

He turned away. Borrowing a friend's cottage or plane was one thing. A wife was something else. No friend was going to be that understanding. Even if the wife was a willing accomplice.

'The police might come back,' he pointed out.

'They might, but not for a while. They were a bit embarrassed about breaking the door down.' She glanced up at him. 'I didn't call them, Gannon.'

'Then why did they turn up mob-handed this morning?'

'Mob-handed? Since when did two

constitute a mob?'

'There might only have been two in the car, but there was definitely a mob in the van that followed them. I only just got out in time. They surrounded the place before they smashed the door in. I heard it go from the copse.'

'They didn't say. The two that were waiting for me.'

'Did they give you a hard time?'

'No. Not really. Not once I'd convinced them that I was who I said I was. But I nearly had kittens when they insisted on coming inside. I thought you were there.'

'What excuse did they make?'

'They said they were checking up on all last night's unexplained alarms. And — '

'And?'

'They seemed to think I might be some kind of accomplice.' She had been about to explain about the confusion over identities. She knew she would have to tell him. After that kiss. She couldn't allow him to think that his friend's wife let just any passing stranger kiss her at the drop of a hat. But not yet. She wasn't quite ready for that. Besides, he might think she was encouraging him to do it again. She rather thought he would be right. 'Or something.'

He glanced at her, then said, 'Of course, they might just know I'm a friend of Richard. In which case his cottage would be the obvious place to look.'

'Do they know who you are? The paper said not.'

'The paper might not know all the details, but the police probably have a good idea. And they may be back. I'm sorry, Dora. I've caused you an awful lot of bother.'

'You'd better just add me to your list of friends. Then you won't worry about it. And you needn't worry about the police either. We're not going to stay at the cottage. I'm just going back to secure the place, then we're going to my flat in London.'

Her flat? Why hadn't she said *our* flat? They'd reached the car, and he waited while she unlocked it and then, pushing the bags onto the floor, settled Sophie in the back.

'There's a doll in one of the bags. Why don't you give it to her?' she suggested.

He found the little rag doll and tucked it in Sophie's hands. She looked at Dora, smiled shyly and muttered a few words. She dredged her memory and found herself saying the Grasnian equivalent of 'you're welcome'.

'Where the hell did you learn that?' Gannon demanded, suspicion jagging across his features.

She shrugged a little awkwardly. 'I've been to Grasnia. I understand what you're trying to do and I sympathise. Truly. You don't have to lie to me.' Then, 'For God's sake, get in before you collapse.' He headed for the driver's door, but she stood her ground. 'I'm driving.' He gave her a thoughtful look but didn't argue, instead climbing into the passenger seat, where he sat bunched up, his knees practically touching his chin, dripping all over the place. 'You can slide the seat back a bit more,' she said. It slid back an inch or two.

She shrugged apologetically, strapped herself in and set off at a brisk pace down the lane, pulling up outside the cottage a few minutes later. 'You'd better dry off and change your clothes while I try and secure the door.'

He didn't waste any time, and when he returned she had just retrieved the mobile phone and was about to punch in a number. He stared at her, but she ignored him and carried on.

'Sarah? It's Dora. How's Laurie?' Sarah would have discussed her infant offspring's wellbeing, cleverness and beauty at length, but Dora didn't have the time. 'Wonderful. Give her a kiss for me. Sarah, darling, I wonder if you could do something for me? I've had a bit of an accident with the front door of the cottage. It needs a carpenter and someone to sort out the lock. Rather urgently. And the phone's out of order, too.' She smiled at Gannon. 'Bless you, darling. Send me the bill.' She finished the call and looked at Gannon thoughtfully. 'Have you met Sarah?'

'Richard's sister? Once.'

'She's a great fixer. You should have called on her.'

'I didn't plan on calling on anybody, Dora.'

'Anyone who's in as much trouble as you seem to be needs all the help he can get. Shall we go?'

He was a terrible passenger. He winced continually as she sped along the motorway and practically made a hole in the floor with his foot, shadow braking as she whizzed through the London traffic. She took no notice. But when he yelped as she took on a black cab at the Hyde Park roundabout and won, she leaned forward and quite deliberately turned up the radio.

After that he took the hint, but long before they reached her flat he had closed his eyes.

'Okay, Gannon. It's safe to come out now,' she said, having whipped into a space between a Mercedes and a Jaguar, missing them both by inches.

He murmured something that might have been a prayer of thanks. Or then again, maybe not. 'Do you always drive like that?'

'Like what?' Her expression was pure innocence, and it didn't fool Gannon for a minute. Dora Marriott, or Kavanagh, or whatever she liked to call herself, was about as innocent as sin. And probably as much fun. A memory of warm lips, the honeyed taste of her tongue returned to taunt him. Not probably. There was no doubt about it. But forbidden fun.

'Come on, sweetheart.' She had tilted her seat forward and was coaxing Sophie out of the back of the car. The trouble was that Sophie had spent the entire journey sorting through the bags of clothes and trying on anything that she could get on, none of it done up properly.

'I'd better carry her,' Gannon said.

'Nonsense. She's fine.' She set the child down on the pavement. 'Well, maybe not *fine*,' she giggled as the dungarees promptly fell down and she noticed that the trainers were on the wrong feet.

'She managed the coat.'

Dora picked her up and hugged her. 'She looks gorgeous. I'll take her, if you can bring the bags.'

'Good afternoon, Miss Kavanagh,' the porter said, as they swept into the entrance lobby like refugees from a jumble sale. 'Can I offer you some assistance?'

'No. We're fine, Brian. But if you could manage to find me a pint of milk, I'd be grateful.'

'No problem. I'll bring it up with your post. Since you seem to have your hands full.'

'Thank you.'

'And, Brian . . . if anyone asks for me I'm not at home, and you don't know where I am.'

'Mr Fergus Kavanagh has been looking for you, miss. He's called several times. I think he suspected you were at home, miss, but not answering the messages he left on your machine.'

'I'll check them when I get in, but when I said I'm not at home, I meant it. Especially to my brother.'

Brian carefully avoided looking at John Gannon. 'Yes, miss. You won't be disturbed.'

Gannon, looking a little grim, followed her to the lift and pushed back the wrought-iron gate. 'He'll think you're having an affair.'

'Maybe. But he won't tell.'

'You know that from past experience, do you?'

She turned on him. 'God, Gannon, you're bloody rude. I'm already an accessory to whatever crimes you've committed, the least you can do is try to be *polite*.'

'This is a nice place to live,' he said, in an effort to oblige, but Dora simply threw him a look that suggested he wasn't trying hard enough. Maybe that was because his head was bursting with questions, questions that were driving his own problems out of his mind.

'You know, the last time I saw Richard he was struggling with all kinds of financial problems. It was why Elizabeth left him,' Gannon added.

'She left him because she married him for his title and discovered too late there was no money to go with it — at least not the kind she was anticipating. She should have stuck around. Things picked up right after she decided the banker was a better bet.'

'I can see that,' he said, as they stepped out onto the top floor. He dropped the bags inside the hall of the apartment and glanced through the open doorway to where huge picture windows looked out across the river.

In fact he could see that Richard Marriott must be doing very well indeed these days, because it suddenly dawned on him that keeping a wife like Dora had to be a very expensive luxury.

Not that the improvement in his fiscal status had done much to keep his new wife happy. Not if the way she'd thrown herself into that kiss was anything to go by.

7

'What exactly were you doing in Grasnia, Dora?'

They were in the kitchen. Gannon on a high stool, his elbows propped up on the island unit, his hands around a mug of the heart-poundingly strong coffee he had declared an essential restorative after Dora's driving. Dora, her fridge bare of anything that would seriously constitute lunch, even for a child, was searching her cupboards for a can of soup she was sure she had somewhere. Sophie was in the sitting room, trying on each item of clothing and staring in fascination at the television.

'Exactly?' Dora didn't turn around. It was truth time, and she wasn't looking forward to admitting that she had been lying to Gannon — well, not lying exactly, just allowing him to labour under a misapprehension — about her and Richard. She'd been too angry with him to even speak when they'd first arrived in the flat, but she knew she couldn't put it off for much longer. Grasnia was a very welcome diversion.

'Precisely will do, if you prefer.'

'I was on an aid convoy,' she said, finally unearthing the soup and giving the list of ingredients her closest attention. 'Well, three, actually,' she said, turning around when there was no response.

He looked shaken to the core. 'You drove a lorry to Grasnia?'

'Not all the way. We took it in turns to drive.' Then, 'It's all right, Gannon, I didn't use London driving techniques to get around,' she said, assuming it was her driving that was concerning him. 'It wasn't the sort of place to try and cut up the opposition.' Not when the opposition were toting automatic weapons.

But that wasn't what he meant. 'Richard let you go?' he demanded. 'Doesn't he listen to the news? Good grief, Dora, has he any idea of the danger?'

Oh, it was that old thing. The *'What's a sweet girl like you think she's doing getting involved in something nasty, something dangerous, when she could be more usefully occupied having a facial?'* old thing.

John Gannon and her brother should get together and form a duet, she thought. Or maybe a trio, because, to be fair, her brother-in-law hadn't been exactly encouraging either.

'Richard did have a few things to say on the subject,' she admitted. And then Poppy had reminded him very firmly that it was none of his business what her sister did, and besides, he could safely leave all the really heavyweight nagging to Fergus. Raising his two younger sisters after their parents had been killed in an earthquake had, over the years, given him plenty of opportunity to perfect his technique. But on this occasion to little avail.

'Do you think Sophie would like

this?' she asked, showing him a can, delaying the moment of truth just a little longer.

'Sophie isn't fussy. She'll eat anything and be glad to get it.'

Yes, of course she would. 'I'll open it, then. There must be some bread in the freezer.' What on earth was the matter with her? He kept giving her opportunities, so why couldn't she just say the words? *Actually I'm not married to Richard. I'm not married to anyone.* What was so difficult about that?

Because without that barrier there would be nothing to stop him jumping to all the right conclusions about the way she'd kissed him, instead of all the wrong ones, because she had to face it, he hadn't exactly reeled back in horror. Considering she was supposed to be the wife of his very good friend Richard Marriott.

It had already occurred to her that Gannon might actually be just the tiniest bit pleased that she *wasn't* Richard's wife — once she had got around to telling him. He might even be pleased enough to kiss her again. She might even let him.

Might? Her subconscious gave a hollow laugh at such self-delusion as she opened the freezer and dug out a loaf of bread, and a little bubble of excitement rose beneath her breastbone as she remembered the touch of his lips against hers; cold and wet from the rain, they had heated up like steam in a boiler.

Was that knowledge the root of her reluctance to tell him the truth? Because it would be so easy to get carried away, lose her head if he decided to try it again? A fact she was quite sure he was aware of and would use to his own advantage if she let him. And she wasn't kidding herself . . . any man who'd snatch a child, steal a plane, break into a friend's house and kidnap his wife wouldn't think twice about seducing her if he thought it would serve his purpose. At least he wouldn't think twice about it if she was giving him the impression that she might welcome the experience . . .

Okay, so maybe he'd hadn't *exactly* kidnapped her, but he'd certainly kept her prisoner in that bathroom while he'd taken a shower, and any man who would do a thing like that was scarcely over-endowed with scruples, was he? In fact a besotted woman would suit such a man very well indeed. She wouldn't ask so many awkward questions.

And it was right after that kiss that he had stopped arguing and agreed to her plans. Sure that she was on his side. Sure that she wouldn't betray him. Sure that she was putty in his hands.

And at that moment he might well have been right. If it hadn't been for that careless crack about her knowing Brian would keep quiet because she brought strange men home on a regular basis, she would still be putty . . .

But her anger had worked liked a dose of smelling salts, clearing her head, bringing her down to earth. The truth was that except for the fact that he knew her brother-in-law John Gannon was still a complete mystery to her. She didn't know who he was or what kind of trouble he was in.

What kind of trouble *she* was in — because she'd held the forces of law and order at bay for him, lied to them for him ... And now he was in her apartment, at her invitation, and he'd heard her tell Brian to keep everyone away, including Fergus. That had been a mistake. Fergus was just the man she needed — they needed — right now. Because he would certainly know exactly what to do. The only danger being that he might decide calling the police was exactly what to do. He could be right.

Helping take relief supplies into Eastern Europe had been positively sane in comparison with this. Or at least, if not sane, she'd known the risks. But the moment this stranger had stepped over the threshold of the cottage she'd apparently lost what little sense she'd been born with.

'Did you have an argument about it? About driving relief supplies?' Gannon continued. 'Is that why you're sleeping apart?' Dora froze, and it had nothing to do with the cold air spilling out of the freezer and condensing around her feet in the warmth of the kitchen. 'I'm sorry,' he said, almost immediately. 'It's none of my business. Forget I asked.'

She swallowed, guilt heating her skin. *Now. Tell him now.* 'Richard and I . . . Richard isn't . . . '

'I just couldn't help noticing that you weren't using the marital bed,' he added, just when she'd decided to do the decent thing and own up.

Was that what this inquisition was all about? Did he think that since the marriage bed was apparently vacant, and she had made free with everything else, she might just oblige with that too? Could it be that the thought of good old Richard wasn't going to prove quite the restraint that she had hoped?

But then she hadn't behaved quite like a besotted bride when he'd kissed her, had she? Kissing him back had been a bad mistake. Well, it was too late to do anything about that, but she could make sure it wasn't repeated.

She slammed the freezer door shut and swung around. 'You're right, Gannon. It isn't any of your business. You're the one with all the explaining to do.' She put the bread on the counter-top and, using a blunt knife, levered the slices apart. 'Why don't you see if you can do two things at once? While you're explaining what this is all about, you can make yourself useful by opening that can.' That would at least keep his hands busy.

'And you're still using your own name,' he said, totally ignoring her demand for some answers. His gaze strayed to her left hand, bare of rings. 'I know, it's not compulsory. But you don't really strike me as a hard-line feminist.' Unfortunately it was not as easy to keep his mouth occupied. The only way she could think of was definitely off limits.

'Really? And what do I strike you as?' *Wrong, wrong. You're just playing into his hands that way.* But she was human enough to want to know.

'I'm still working on that one.'

She might have guessed. He hadn't yet given her a straight answer to the simplest of questions. 'Well, let me know when you've come to a conclusion. It will be a pleasure to tell you just how far off the mark you are.'

For a moment their eyes locked in a battle of wills, then Gannon slid off the stool, picked up the can and, still looking at her, slowly opened it.

There was speculation in that look. Something knowing that curled up her insides, and she knew she'd been right not to tell him the truth. Okay, so he suspected her 'marriage' might be in trouble. But at least he still thought she *was* married. To a man he claimed as a friend. So he wouldn't do anything silly, would he? Not unless she encouraged him. And she wasn't about to do that.

The kiss in the woods didn't count. It

hadn't started out as anything more than an attempt to hide her face from Mrs Fuller. And they could both hide behind fear and adrenalin for the way it turned out. If they were sensible. *Ha!*

If only she knew more about him, why he needed her help. So far she had relied on her instincts to guide her, and her instincts had told her that, despite all the evidence to the contrary, he was on the side of the angels. But then women had been fooling themselves that way since the Fall. Maybe she was just fooling herself now.

He hadn't been exactly brimming over with confidences, and he had simply countered her questions with his own. Side-tracking her. Keeping his secrets.

Good grief, this was the classic situation of every woman-in-peril thriller. If she'd been watching this on the cinema screen she would have been urging the stupid woman to call the police, get out of there, run . . .

And she couldn't say she hadn't been

warned. From the very first day at nursery school one thing had been drummed into them all . . . *never talk to strangers.* Okay, so Gannon hadn't offered her sweets . . . or had he? That kiss had been sugared almonds and jelly babies and chocolate buttons all rolled into one. And everyone knew how addictive chocolate was.

She was seriously regretting instructing Brian not to tell her brother she was home. Fergus might read her the riot act endlessly for her stupidity, and check up on her every move for the next ten years because of this madness, but he only did it because he loved her, wanted to protect her . . .

Well, maybe it wasn't too late to call him. Gannon had trusted her sufficiently to let her go out and get some clothes for Sophie. Surely he wouldn't object to a trip to the local shop to stock up the fridge? They had to eat.

'I'm going to have to go out and buy some food,' she said.

'The freezer looked pretty well stocked to me.'

'We need eggs, cheese, milk,' she snapped out. 'And some orange juice for Sophie.' *The evening newspaper might not be such a bad idea, either.* 'Maybe she should have some vitamins, too. And I wasn't planning on waiting for something to defrost before we ate. It's been a long time since breakfast. You must be hungry.'

'I've known worse.'

'In Grasnia?'

'There and other places. Until recently I was a foreign correspondent for a news agency. Wars a speciality.' He regarded her with something close to, but not quite, a smile. 'In case you were wondering.'

'And what are you now?'

'I'm self-employed . . . at least where trouble is concerned.'

'You said it, Gannon. So you'd better stay here and feed Sophie while I go and shop.'

'Actually, I really don't think that's

such a good idea, Dora.'

'I won't be long,' she said, hoping the tremor in her limbs wasn't transmitting itself to her voice. She hadn't seriously considered the possibility of him keeping her locked up in her own apartment. Hadn't she done enough to convince him that she was on his side? Whatever side that was.

'How long does it take?' She wasn't sure what he meant by that, and it must have shown on her face because he decided to explain. 'The last time you went shopping the police arrived in force,' he reminded her.

Dora was outraged. 'I told you that was nothing to do with me — and you're not the only one in trouble, Gannon. I *lied* to them for you.'

'And now you're having second thoughts about it. I don't blame you, Dora, but you'll understand my reticence about letting you out of my sight again. If you need supplies, I'm sure your friendly hall porter would be only too happy to help. You might ask him to get you a copy of the evening newspaper, too. Just in case I've made the front page.'

'Is that likely?' she demanded, appalled at the prospect. 'If you have he'll recognise you.' And he'd be the one calling the police. That possibility should have made her feel better. But oddly it didn't.

His smile was a touch wry. 'I doubt that, somehow.' He rubbed the palm of his hand over his chin. 'I'm not exactly looking my best.'

She attempted a careless shrug. 'Whatever. I'll go down and ask him.'

He wasn't so easily fooled. 'Why don't you save energy and use the internal telephone?' He lifted the receiver and offered it to her.

It seemed he was serious, deadly serious, about not letting her out of his sight again. She swallowed nervously. 'Have you already disconnected the outside line?' she enquired. He'd been all around the apartment, checking the lay-out.

'No. I'll need the telephone.'

'To call up more of your understanding friends?' She put all the disdain she
could muster into her voice. But it was
too little and much too late.

'A man needs all the friends he can
get. Maybe you should call Richard,
too,' he suggested. 'Just in case he's
wondering where you are. Or have
things got so bad that you aren't even
speaking?' He held up his hands in a
defensive gesture as she glared at him.
'All right, I know. It's none of my
business. But he was a good friend
when I needed him. And one failed
marriage is enough for anyone.'

'Are you speaking from personal
experience, here?'

'No. That's one of the few mistakes
I've yet to make. But I saw what it did
to Richard.'

'You don't have to worry about him,
Gannon. Richard is as happy as any
man has a right to be,' she declared
roundly.

'You can guarantee that, can you?'

'Stick around and ask him. I don't think he'll disagree with my assessment of his state of mind. I'd call him and let him tell you himself, but I can't, he's travelling about all the time. I don't know where he is from one day to the next.'

'And he doesn't call you?'

'He's probably been trying the cottage,' she said, without so much as a twinge of conscience, her every good intention about telling him the truth on hold. The only information prisoners were obliged to part with was name, rank and number. He had all that, and more. At least he thought he had, and she'd done enough fool things in the last few hours without making things worse. 'Of course he won't be able to get through,' she added.

Gannon wasn't in the least bit apologetic. 'What about the mobile?' he asked.

That was the trouble when you started improvising. Things just got out of hand. 'It's new.' She said the first thing that came into her head. 'He doesn't have the number. Maybe he'll call Sarah, and she'll tell him I'm here.'

'You didn't tell Sarah that you were coming here,' he pointed out.

'Didn't I? Well, she'll guess. Or he will.'

'Whatever you say,' he replied evenly, clearly not believing a word. He was still holding the telephone receiver, and once more he offered it to her. 'So, are you going to give Brian a call?'

'Do I have a choice?'

'I'm afraid not.'

Rather than face the dark, searching challenge of his eyes another moment, she snatched the receiver from him and turned her back on him as she pressed the button to call the porter. He responded instantly.

'Brian? It's Dora Kavanagh. Can you ask the corner shop to send me some groceries, please? I'll give you a list.'

Gannon watched her as she told the man what she wanted. She was rattled. On edge. Well, it was hardly surprising;

she'd been through a lot in the last few hours. He'd put her through a lot.

Until now she'd scarcely batted an eyelid. But suddenly she was nervous.

He'd have liked to be able to pretend that he didn't know why. But he'd spent too many years studying people who were trying to hide their feelings to get off that easily. She had changed from the moment when he had kissed her on that muddy path and she had kissed him back. He wondered what had bothered her the most; that in a moment of madness she had betrayed her husband, or the realisation that given the chance she would do it again?

She'd been quiet on the drive into London, but he hadn't had time to worry about it then; he'd been too busy worrying about whether they would reach their destination in one piece, worrying how long it would be before the pain got too bad for him to keep going. But ever since the front door of her apartment had closed behind them she had become increasingly edgy.

She was ready to bolt given half a chance, and he couldn't allow that. Sophie needed her. *And you need her, too.* He tried to ignore the insistent voice in his head, but it wouldn't go away. *You want her.*

His fingers curled around the edge of the counter-top. He wanted her more than any woman he had ever met. Even now, looking at her as she concentrated on remembering everything she might want for the next day or two, his guts were being twisted like spaghetti round a fork, with the kind of longing he thought he'd left behind with all his other illusions.

It should have been like all the lights in the world coming on at once. But it wasn't. Richard was his friend; Dora was his friend's wife. There would be no angels singing the 'Hallelujah Chorus' for him, just the bleak prospect of doing the right thing and walking away the moment that he'd sorted this mess out. But not yet. He couldn't go yet. Not while his ribs were giving him hell, while Sophie's future was in any doubt.

'There.' She hung up and turned defiantly to face him. 'That should do it.'

'It certainly should. You've laid in sufficient supplies for the five thousand.'

She shrugged. 'Well, you never know when the five thousand might drop by, probably all of them wearing policemen's helmets. In the meantime, since that soup won't heat itself, I'll do it, shall I? And while I look after Sophie you can make your phone calls.'

'You're that keen to get rid of me? Well, I can't say I blame you. I promise I won't stay a second longer than necessary.'

'I don't exactly have a choice, do I?' Not that she wanted him to go. Despite all her doubts, she wasn't in the business of lying to herself. What she really wanted was to touch him, hold him, make everything right for him, and she'd never felt that way about anyone before in her entire life. It made her feel vulnerable, at the mercy of feelings she didn't understand. Or maybe she did understand them, all too well. She just didn't want to acknowledge the fact. 'But I don't like being on the wrong side of the law, Gannon,' she said curtly. 'I want things sorted out. For Sophie's sake as well as my own.'

'Then we have the same objective.'

'Good. So you won't mind if I call my doctor and have him give her a thorough check-up, will you?' She turned and looked at him, and despite her anger her heart turned over.

There was a greyness about his skin, a pinched look around his mouth from pain — pain that he was refusing to acknowledge. He should see a doctor too, she knew, but she didn't say anything. She'd leave that argument until she had the doctor to back her up.

'Actually, that's not a bad idea.' She almost collapsed from the shock. It must have shown on her face because he almost smiled. 'I need to organise a

201

blood test,' he said. 'The sooner the better.'

'A blood test?'

'Don't look so concerned. I just need to be able to prove that Sophie is my daughter, establish that she has a right to be here.'

His daughter! 'Your daughter? But I thought — '

'You thought she was just some refugee I'd whisked out of the country without proper papers?'

'Something like that,' she mumbled.

'Because the same thing crossed your mind when you were out there?' Her eyes slid away. She'd wanted to, she was still ashamed to be part of a world that left children to suffer so. 'I know how difficult it is to leave the children. Believe me, I know. But it is for the best. Their country will need them, every one of them — '

Her head came up. 'If they survive.'

'They will.' He reached out, touched her cheek with just the tip of his fingers, and she jumped, physically jumped, as the contact fizzed against her skin like a tiny electric shock. Gannon curled his fingers into a loose fist, as if it was the only way of controlling them, before letting his hand fall to his side. 'With people like you on their side.'

'If that's so, why didn't you leave Sophie with her mother?' she challenged him.

'It wasn't possible.'

'Why?'

'Leave it, Dora,' he said irritably. 'It's history. Is that soup ready yet?'

She stared at him for a moment longer, then turned back to the saucepan and switched off the heat. 'Just about. Can you put a couple of slices of bread in the toaster while I fetch Sophie?'

Sophie had settled on a dark blue T-shirt, a pair of trousers that were a shade too long and, despite the grey, miserable weather, a sunhat. Now she was sitting on the floor, switching the television from one channel to another with the remote control, staring in fascination as cartoons, old movies, a golf tournament and a talk show followed one another across the screen in rapid succession.

Dora took the remote from her, settled on a cartoon and then bent to roll up the child's trousers before finding a pair of socks and trainers from the heap. The effort required to get her into them as Sophie dived around, determined not to miss a second of the cartoon, at least helped to blot out the endless questions racing through her head. Briefly. That done, she took Sophie off to wash her hands, resorting to picking her up and carrying her when encouragement didn't work.

Dora could see she was already ten times better than she had been last night. Food, warmth and antibiotics were all doing a good job. But she still wanted her looked at by a professional.

And she still wanted some answers. Particularly about Sophie's mother. She wanted to know what had happened to her, and, history or not, she wouldn't be put off for ever.

She had just reached the kitchen when the telephone began to ring.

She paused, looked uncertainly at Gannon.

'Aren't you going to answer that?' he asked.

'The machine's on. Whoever it is will leave a message.' *And please, please don't let them say anything to undermine her story.* She picked up Sophie and popped her onto a stool, handed her a spoon, all the time trying desperately hard not to listen while her voice invited her caller to leave a message.

'Dora? It's Richard. I just spoke to Sarah and she said there had been some bother at the cottage, that you'd left in a bit of a hurry — '

Before she could even turn, Gannon had crossed the hall and picked up the telephone. 'Richard. This is John — John Gannon — '

'*John?*' There was a pause while Richard absorbed this information.

'What the devil are you doing in Dora's apartment?'

'I'm afraid that I'm the bother.' Gannon turned and looked at Dora, white-faced across the hall in the kitchen. 'I broke into your cottage last night because I needed somewhere quiet to stay for a few days. I had no idea it was occupied — '

'Good grief, John, you must have scared poor Dora out of her wits.'

'Not half as much as she scared me.' He was silent for a moment while his knuckles whitened as he clutched at the receiver. 'I understand congratulations are in order. I didn't know you'd remarried.'

'What? Oh, yes. At Christmas. I'd have had you as best man if I'd known what country you were in. I'll bore you at length about how happy I am when I get back from the States — if you'll still be around?'

'My wandering days are over, Richard. I look forward to seeing you.' His voice had a struggle to get past the hard lump in his throat. It barely made it. He forced himself to repeat the words, with conviction. 'I look forward to it.'

'Great. So tell me, John, what have you been up to that you were forced to hide out at the cottage? Woman trouble?'

'Something like that. Let's just say that my place is off limits until I've sorted out one or two things. Dora kindly offered to put me and my daughter up for a few days . . . I hope you don't mind.'

'Why should I mind if Dora doesn't? What — ?' Before Gannon could think of an answer, Richard had put his hand over the receiver briefly, turning away to have a muffled conversation with someone. 'Look, I've got to go, John. We'll catch up on all the news when I get back. You've obviously got plenty. A *daughter*, did you say?'

'Yes — '

'Well, whatever kind of mess you're in, Dora's your girl. She's got serious guts, and she knows everybody. I'll see you when I get back, John.'

'Don't you want to speak — ?' But he was talking to the dialling tone.

He replaced the receiver with extreme care on the cradle. Richard Marriott was a man he had looked up to and admired all his life. He'd seen him on the rack when one marriage failed and put the blame on Elizabeth without question. But suddenly he wondered if he had been right. Any man who was that casual with his wife scarcely deserved her love and loyalty, let alone the kind of happiness that he boasted of.

Dora was waiting, poised, expectant across the hall, yet with something, apprehension almost, clouding her eyes. 'Richard sent you his love,' he said, putting all the feeling he could dredge up into the words.

'Did he?' She very much doubted it. He was just saying what he thought she'd want to hear. Protecting her from disappointment. It was oddly touching.

'He was called away,' Gannon went on, his hands curling with the effort it took not to cross the room, take her in his arms and hold her, love her as she should be loved instead of making excuses for her husband. No meeting could be that important. 'He didn't seem to mind that I was staying here,' he added.

'Why should he?' Dora asked, pushing her luck a little, still unable to quite believe that she'd got away with it. 'You're his friend.'

'That's what he said. He obviously trusts you . . . and me . . . '

'He's no reason not to.' For just a second their gaze met, and Dora felt a charge of heat light up her insides as they both remembered the moment in the woods when neither of them had been thinking about Richard. In her case it was understandable. In his . . . well, it seemed that Gannon was having a little trouble deciding whether to be saint or sinner.

The doorbell rang and he peeled away, releasing her from the intensity of his searching gaze so that her breath came back in a rush and her legs quite suddenly didn't have sufficient strength to hold her, so that she had to hang onto the counter top.

The reprieve was all too brief. 'The guy at the door wants some money for the food mountain he's brought.'

'It's in my handbag.' There was the slightest wobble in her voice. 'Help yourself.'

Once again their eyes met briefly over Sophie's head. 'I don't think that's such a good idea, Dora,' Gannon said, his own voice tight in his throat. 'You never know where an invitation like that might lead.' And he passed the bag to her.

8

'Where are you going, Dora?'

Dora shouldered Sophie and stood her ground. 'Sophie almost fell asleep over her soup. I thought I'd put her down for a nap. Any objections?' she demanded, when Gannon continued to block the kitchen doorway, a box of groceries in his arms. Then, 'She didn't get much sleep last night.'

'No, I suppose not.' He struggled to contain a yawn that caught him out. 'None of us did.'

'The spare room is the one on the right. Help your — ' Dora bit back the words. He acknowledged her mistake with one of those lazy, economical smiles that lit up something inside his face and turned the lights on inside her. The kind of smile that curled her toes and threatened an emotional chain reaction that could so easily wipe out her determination to keep her distance. 'You're most welcome to use it,' she said, with careful politeness.

'Thank you,' he replied, mocking her. 'But I've got a few things to do before I can take a nap.' He stepped aside, and Dora felt rather than saw him catch his breath as his damaged ribs grated together, and she shuddered as her own body seemed to echo the sickening sensation.

'There are some painkillers in the drawer. They might help,' she said, on a sharp breath. 'Or maybe you'd rather wait for the doctor to prescribe you something stronger?'

'I don't need anything,' he muttered, sweat standing out on his brow. 'Just you to move out of the way so that I can put the siege rations down.'

She would have taken them from him, but burdened with Sophie, half asleep on her shoulder, she was unable to do more than step out of his way, glancing back as he crossed the kitchen.

Unaware that she was still watching

him, Gannon slumped against the island unit, his breathing shallow as he fought to control the pain. He was hurting a lot more than she had realised, certainly more than he would ever admit to, and she wanted, needed to go to him, take him in her arms and hold him until the hurt went away.

Before she could do anything, however, he quite deliberately straightened, his teeth clenched against the pain, and she stepped out of sight before he turned and caught her staring at him. He was a man who lived on his strength, and she knew he would hate her to see him kitten-weak, even for a moment. But as she moved quickly down the hall she was more determined than ever that the doctor should see him, too.

She laid the sleepy child on her bed and pulled off her shoes, socks and trousers before brushing her hair out of her eyes and tucking the quilt around her, taking time to recover from the racketing heat of her pulse, time to remind herself of all the good reasons not to open her heart. It was getting harder each time.

'I'll call the doctor now,' she said, returning to the kitchen. Gannon turned to look at her, and all her hard-won determination to keep her distance evaporated. The greyness of his skin had intensified and his face had the pinched look of a man near the end of his tether. 'John?' she murmured uncertainly.

For a moment he remained perfectly still. Then he turned and pushed past her, and a moment later she heard him retching painfully. She hesitated. She longed to go to him, hold his head, bathe it, cradle him. Only the certainty that he would rather not have a witness to his weakness kept her rooted to the spot.

There was a long moment of silence, and, suddenly afraid that he had passed out, she began to run. Then she heard water running as he turned on the taps, and she stopped with her hand on the door. He didn't need her this time. But she could do the next best thing and call the doctor, tell him that he had two patients to look at and ask him to come as quickly as he could.

She had just replaced the receiver when she realised that he was standing in the doorway and she spun around. 'You'd better sit down before you fall down, Gannon,' she said tightly.

For a moment she thought he was going to argue. Then he threw up a hand in what could only be a gesture of resignation. 'You could be right,' he said, crossing slowly to the nearest armchair and lowering himself cautiously into it. 'Remind me never to let you drive me anywhere again.'

'Oh, I see, that was travel sickness, was it?' she asked, with teasing sarcasm that nearly choked her.

'What else?' he said, and clutched at his chest, holding himself together as he was shaken by a coughing spasm.

What else indeed? The kind of travel sickness that occurs when the journey ends somewhat abruptly in a field. The kind of travel sickness that you get when you ignore cracked ribs and make a run for it with a child in your arms. The kind of travel sickness that could get very complicated indeed without medical attention. 'I think I'll wait for the doctor to make a diagnosis if you don't mind,' she said.

'You've called him?'

'Of course I've called him. I'm in enough trouble without having to explain away the body of a strange man in my flat.'

'I'm not about to expire, Dora. I just need to rest for a while.'

'Is that all? You'll have to forgive my lack of confidence, but I'm the one over here looking at you, and frankly I think it's going to take more than a nap to put you right.'

He squeezed his eyes shut, pinching the bridge of his nose between his thumb and long, slender fingers. 'Maybe you're right. But before I can think about a trip to Casualty for an

X-ray I should make some calls, too.'

'I agree. And a solicitor should be at the top of your list. I can give you name of a good one, if it'll help?'

'Thanks, but I have my own. But you wouldn't happen to have a friend in the Home Office, would you? Richard said you know a lot of people.'

She frowned. 'Did he?' If Richard had said that, he obviously assumed that she was helping Gannon out of his difficulties and clearly saw nothing wrong in that. 'Actually, he's right. In fact I met the Home Secretary himself once, at a dinner party — '

Gannon raised his eyebrows. 'Did you, by God? Well, perhaps we shouldn't bother the boss just yet.' He offered a smile. 'Better keep him in reserve, just in case. For the moment I'd be quite happy with someone at Principal Secretary level. Just as long as he's friendly.'

'Would a friendly *female* Principal Secretary do?' It was his turn to lift an eyebrow. 'Not all my friends are male. Nor are all civil servants, come to that.'

'I'm not prejudiced, Dora. I don't care about the sex, just as long as he, she or it is likely to be sympathetic.'

'That probably depends on just how many laws you've broken — '

'I wasn't counting.'

'And, more importantly, which ones.'

He shrugged. 'Let's see. There's removing a child from a refugee camp without permission — I'm not quite sure what law that breaks, but there's bound to be one.'

'Several, I should think.'

'Then there is the small detail of smuggling her across more international borders than I can at this moment recall.'

'Borrowing a plane without the owner's permission?' Her prompt was greeted by a fleeting smile.

'Thank you, Dora, I hadn't forgotten that one, but Henri won't press charges once I've had a chance to explain. Making an unauthorised landing, entering the country without informing Immigration or Customs and Excise, and bringing in an illegal alien might, however, prove a little more problematical — '

'I imagine it will.' She waited, then, when he didn't offer any further misdemeanours, she asked, 'Is that it?'

'All I can think of. Apart from breaking and entering, of course. But you already know about that one. Will *you* press charges, Dora?'

'Don't get smart with me, Gannon. I'm already an accessory after the fact in that one. I meant drugs, smuggling of dutiable goods, possession of illegal firearms — serious stuff. If I'm going to ask friends for favours I need to know that you're not . . . ' A crook. Using Sophie as a shield. Using me. He was looking at her with a slightly detached expression, as if he knew exactly what was coming next but was damned if he was going to help her out with the words. She gave an awkward little shrug. 'Well, I don't know a whole lot about you,' she finished, somewhat lamely.

'I just wanted to get my daughter to safety, Dora. Bring her home. If you've any doubts about that, you'd be well advised to pick up the telephone again and call the police right now.'

Dora was perplexed. 'But if she's your daughter, Gannon, why didn't you just go through the proper channels?'

'Do you think I didn't try that first?' He leaned back in the chair, with every appearance of a man at the end of his tether. 'Have you any idea how long it would have taken? Most of the people at the camp just thought I'd taken a fancy to the child, wanted to give her a chance. Some thought I was trying to get her out for adoption by a couple desperate for a child. And they were the charitable ones. No one actually believed that I was telling the truth, and she wasn't in the kind of place you can get a genetic blood match at the drop of a hat, you know.'

'No, I suppose not. But taking her was — '

'An act of desperation? I *was*

220

desperate. It was that or leave her there while the wheels of bureaucracy ground ever so slowly.' Despite the pain and weariness, his look was suddenly razor-sharp. 'You wouldn't have left her there, would you, Dora?'

She had the feeling that he was pushing her into an admission that she would have done what he did, that they were cut from the same cloth. Maybe he was right, maybe pushed to the limits she would have done exactly what he did, but under the circumstances it seemed madness to admit it, 'They'll know you took her, won't they?'

'Of course they'll know. It's why I took Henri's plane. I'd never have got through Immigration with her. And I couldn't ask him to break the law and fly me in himself.'

'You didn't care about involving me,' she declared, leaping to her feet, suddenly very angry indeed.

'That's not true, Dora, you involved yourself. You had any number of opportunities to get away and you didn't take them. Remember that when you're being cautioned by the local constabulary.'

'Cautioned?' She stared at him. 'What will they charge me with?'

'I've no idea. But I'm sure they'll think of something. Unless we can sort everything out first. How friendly is this girl you know at the Home Office?'

'Very friendly at a dinner party, or a first night, or the kind of charity function that we both seem to go to. But this is unexplored territory; I can't guarantee that she won't go straight to Immigration if I call her. She'll have her job to think of. In retrospect, I don't think calling her would be that bright.'

'Maybe you're right. But I'm going to have to talk to someone. And soon.'

'I think you should talk to your lawyer first. He might be able to apply for some kind of temporary papers until you can prove Sophie has a right to be here.' She paused. 'Of course you could use your newspaper contacts. Once you've got the tabloids on your side they'll have the whole country weeping into their cornflakes.'

'Thanks, but I don't want that kind of publicity.'

Not even if it meant keeping Sophie safe? Or had he got something to hide?
'I have a certain amount of sympathy with that attitude, but it might help when you're arrested.'

'You think they'll lock me up and throw away the key?'

'It's difficult to know exactly what they'll do — you've broken international laws. And it's very possible that the Grasnians will demand that she's sent back to her mother — '

'Her mother is dead, Dora.'

Dead. The word was so hollow, so empty. So *nothing*. Dora cast round her, as if searching for words that would mean something. That would offer some comfort. All her fumbling brain could offer were platitudes, and besides, what he needed was practical help.

'Can you prove it?' she asked.

Relief flooded through Gannon. She

hadn't asked how. Or why. The questions to which there were no answers. Neither had she asked whether he had loved the woman who had carried his child, or even if she was his wife. But she would. Sooner or later. She wouldn't be able to help herself. And when he told her the whole story — would she be so happy to help him then?

'I don't have a death certificate, if that's what you mean. I don't even know where she's buried. I just have a scribbled note from someone who was with her when she died, a woman who sent on the letter she'd written begging me to take care of Sophie.'

The thought that flew to her mind was a terrible one, and Dora hesitated to voice it, but she knew enough, had seen enough to understand that in a war zone anything could happen. 'You're certain that she is your child, Gannon?'

He'd asked himself that a thousand times as he'd searched for Sophie. Not that it had mattered. A dead woman's plea would have been enough. All he'd known was that the child was in a refugee camp, the woman who had sent him the note had told him that much. But her letter had taken months to reach him and everything had moved on . . . changed . . . And then one day he had walked into a camp and seen this tiny, dark-haired child and he'd known her. But who would believe that? 'I have a photograph of my own mother aged about two. Sophie is the image of her.'

Dora nodded. 'That will help.'

'A blood test will be proof positive. When will your doctor get here?'

'He's taking surgery at the moment. It'll be an hour or so. Can I get you something to eat?'

He shook his head. 'I don't think I'll risk it for a while. I'll just ring my lawyer and then lie down for a while.'

She didn't press him, but left him to make his call while she made up the spare bed. He needed sleep more than food. And once he was asleep maybe she would be able to make some decisions of her own about who *she* should talk to.

Maybe a call to her own lawyer wouldn't be a bad idea, if only to warn him that he might have to bail her out at short notice and get Sophie into the safekeeping of Fergus and his housekeeper. Her brother might be disapproving but he wouldn't let her down in a crisis.

She wished momentarily that she had her sister's number in the States. Then decided she was glad she didn't. She'd taken John Gannon on trust. He hadn't told her everything, but she was sure that what he had told her was the truth. Of course she might be fooling herself, but she knew that checking up on him would make her feel distinctly grubby.

She was shaking the quilt into its cover when she looked up to discover that she was being watched by her unexpected house guest. How long had he been there, those eyes full of secrets levelled at her, seeing into her very soul while giving nothing away? 'All sorted?' she asked brightly.

'Yes.' He dragged his hand over his face. 'He'll clear up the legal position regarding Sophie, make certain that she can stay here while I take steps to prove her right to be here. And he's getting in touch with Henri and sorting out repairs for the plane. Once that's done, we'll go to the local police station together and I'll make a statement. Apparently I'll be charged, and then it will be up to the local magistrate to decide what happens next. Any bets on that one?' he asked.

'You haven't hurt anyone,' she said.

'No. But I have broken a hell of a lot of laws. Earnshaw seems to think I'll have to be made an example of; if they don't, everyone will think they can get away with it.'

'In that case you'd better put in some serious time on this good mattress. Police cells are not comfortable places.'

'You'd know about that, of course?'

The crease at the corner of his mouth that wasn't quite a smile was back.

She shrugged. 'You know how it is.'

'No. Tell me.'

'I once thought I'd like to be an actress, and I managed to get a tiny part in a cop show on TV. I spent the entire time in the 'cells'. Let me tell you, it put me off the whole idea of a career in television. It's far too uncomfortable.'

'What *did* you do for a living?' She didn't have much trouble looking puzzled. 'You said you met Richard through work.'

'No, I said I met him through my sister. She met him through work. She's a model. You might have heard of her — Poppy Kavanagh?'

'I don't spend a lot of time reading fashion magazines.' Then he frowned. 'Do you look like her?'

'A bit. She's taller, and a hell of a lot more glamorous, of course — '

'Maybe I've seen her photograph somewhere.' He started a shrug, but as his ribs kicked in with a reminder of what he'd put them through he had second thoughts. 'I was sure your face was familiar — '

'That must be it.' She'd had her own photograph in the papers quite a bit during the last six months, but she was quite happy for him to think that he'd seen her sister. 'She was on a photo-shoot on the river — at that little bridge near the cottage — when they all got caught in a thunderstorm,' she rattled on quickly. 'Richard was down there working on the cottage, and invited them all in to take shelter.'

'And she introduced you?'

'Mmm.' She and Poppy had shared the flat until then. But the day she'd met Richard, Poppy had moved in with him. She'd only come home to pack. Maybe love at first sight was a family thing. Dora turned away from him, sure that he would see the same desperate, almost reckless longing that she had seen in Poppy's face when she had been throwing her clothes into suitcases, begrudging the time it was taking, time she could have been with Richard.

She tossed the quilt over the bed with a briskness she was far from feeling, tucking the pillows into their cases with a ferocity that betrayed her need.

'There, that should do you. Are you sure you won't try a couple of pain-killers?' she said, when what she really wanted to do was lie beside him, take his pain into her own body, cradle his head against her breast while he slept.

'I don't think anything you can buy at the local pharmacy is likely to do much good, Dora.'

Something in his voice suggested he wasn't talking about painkillers either, and, unable to help herself, she turned, hugging a pillow against her as she tucked it beneath the flap. But whatever she had heard in his voice he had kept from his face. Or maybe she was just hearing what she longed to hear, but had effectively forbidden him from saying.

'Oh, well, I'm sure the doctor will

prescribe something if you ask him. Just try and get some sleep now. There's no need to worry about Sophie, I'll take care of her.' Still he hesitated in the doorway, uncertainty shadowing his eyes. 'Trust me, Gannon. I'm not going anywhere. This problem is mine now, as well as yours.'

After a moment he nodded, and began to unbutton his shirt. Dora's mouth dried as the cloth parted to reveal the smooth, sun-darkened skin of his throat, the scattering of dark hair across his chest. Looking up from the cuffs, he realised that she hadn't moved and he stopped. 'I really appreciate your concern, Dora, but I think it might be better if you left me to handle this part all by myself,' he said.

She blushed beetroot, dropped the pillow onto the bed and fled.

* * *

Sophie stirred a while later, a little grizzly and wanting her father. Dora cuddled her, taking her through to the kitchen to give her some milk and biscuits. Seeking some way to amuse the child, she had just decided to let her help make some little cakes for tea when Brian buzzed up to tell her Dr Croft had arrived, insisting he had been asked to call.

'Oh, sorry, Brian, I should have let you know I was expecting him. Send him up, will you?'

The doctor checked Sophie, looked at the antibiotics she was taking, and then over the top of his half-moon spectacles at Dora. 'Where did you get these?'

'Is there something wrong with them?'

'No. But they weren't dispensed by Boots, were they?' He tapped the UN logo on the label 'What is she? One of your little refugees?'

'Does it matter?'

'Not to me.' He glanced at Sophie and gave her a smile. 'The child has obviously had a chest infection, but these are dealing with it,' he said, putting the bottle down. 'She's a bit underweight, but she seems healthy enough apart from that.' Then he gave Dora a thoughtful look. 'Maybe, in view of her recent living conditions, you should bring her down to the surgery in a day or two. I'll get my nurse to organise a few tests. Just as a precaution.'

'Thank you. Actually, I wanted to ask you about blood tests. Genetic blood tests. Her father needs to prove paternity.'

'Ah. He's my other patient, I take it? Where is he?'

'Resting. He's got cracked ribs that are giving him a lot of pain, he's been sick, and now he's started coughing — '

'Show me.' She led the way to the spare bedroom, tapped on the door and opened it. Gannon was asleep. He was stretched out on the bed, naked shoulders all bones and bruises, thick lashes dark against his prominent cheekbones. 'Mmm, he doesn't look very bright, does he? No, don't wake him. Sleep, you know — ' . . . knits up the ravell'd sleave of . . . ' — umm . . . you know.' He cleared his throat. 'It'll do him more good than anything I can give him.'

'You're sure?'

'I'll leave you a script for some painkillers and antibiotics for him, and I'll look in again first thing in the morning. But if you're worried you can ring me at any time and I'll come straight round.'

'And the genetic blood tests?'

'Is it urgent?'

'It is, rather.'

'Yes, well, I'll get back to you as soon as I've made an appointment at the clinic.'

'Thank you, Doctor.'

He paused in the doorway. 'I suppose you know what you're doing, Dora?'

Her smile was wry. 'Whatever gave you that idea?'

He smiled right back. 'No, well, just take sensible precautions. Shall I give your porter that script to get filled for you? It'll save you going out.' He took it from her hand. 'And any worries, any time, call me. I mean it.'

'Thanks.' She closed the door behind her and turned back to Sophie. 'Right, sweetheart. Let's get back to those cakes.'

★ ★ ★

John Gannon woke with the distinct impression that he'd been run over by a tank. Or an armoured personnel carrier at the very least. Except if that had happened he wouldn't be waking up at all.

It was dusk, golden light was streaming in through the windows and he was lying in a bed of such comfort that only the most urgent call of nature would tempt him from it.

He moved cautiously. And as the pain scythed through him he remembered. And with memory came the haunting bittersweet thoughts that had been with him when he had hit the pillow. He glanced at his watch and swore, It was gone eight. Whatever had happened to the doctor?

He swore again as he moved too quickly. He bent to tug on borrowed trousers and was hit by a wave of giddiness. He used the bathroom, splashed cold water onto his overheated face, clung to the basin as nausea choked at him, refusing to give in to his stomach's bucking demands, and eventually it passed.

He crossed the hall to check on Sophie, back in Dora's bed and curled up fast asleep. She was beginning to look cherished, he thought. Her cheeks had lost that pinched look and had a healthy pink tinge to them, her dark hair was clean and shining. He brushed a strand from her face and she stirred, opened her eyes and smiled at him. He bent and kissed the top of her head, tucking her back under the covers. She was so beautiful. Already he loved her more than life itself.

'Gannon?' He turned. Dora was standing in the doorway. 'How are you?'

'Fine.' A spasm of coughing caught him, betraying him, and he moved away from Sophie out into the hall. 'Fairly fine,' he revised, beneath her sceptical look.

She didn't argue, there was no point. He looked terrible and probably felt worse. She took two small pill bottles from her pocket and handed them to him. 'The doctor left you some painkillers and some antibiotics as a precaution against infection.'

'I don't need antibiotics,' he said, stuffing them into his pocket. 'I need a blood test. Why didn't you wake me?'

'He said not to. And he's made an appointment at the clinic for you the day after tomorrow. It was the earliest they could manage.'

'Couldn't he do it?'

She sympathised with his impatience. She'd pleaded for something sooner, but he'd already been given a cancellation. 'It has to be done under controlled conditions. With independent witnesses. Are you hungry?'

The nausea was still too close to risk food. 'Not particularly.'

'Bovril and a water biscuit?' she suggested doubtfully, as she surveyed his pallid complexion.

He laughed, then clutched his side. 'Damn! But you sounded just like my grandmother.'

'Well, grandmothers know a thing or two.' If she were his grandmother she'd scold him for getting himself into such a pickle, put him to bed with a hot water bottle, bathe his face, tuck him in and sit by him all night long. 'Just so long as I don't look like her,' she added, with a touch of acid, in case all those tender feelings were too obviously written in her face.

Maybe the acid should have been stronger, because he reached out and grazed her cheek with the edge of his thumb, sending a tiny thrill of expectation that rippled through her body, tightening her skin so that all she wanted was for him to hold her, love her.

Gannon's fingers slid beneath her hair as if they had a will of their own. Her skin was like silk, warm to the touch, sensuous. And his senses were suddenly filled with her, drowning out the voice of reason, of self-preservation, the voice that said, You cannot have her. She belongs to someone else.

As her perfume filled his nostrils he was lost to reason. He knew exactly how she would feel wrapped about him, whimpering with pleasure as he touched her hot, sweet body; his ears rang with her cries of passion because he could see it all . . . it was there, smoking from her hot grey eyes. Molten desire that was heating his blood as she swayed towards him, tempting him to take her into his arms and self-destruct . . .

9

Gannon snatched back his hand as if burned, clutching his fingers into a fist. 'No, Dora,' he said, his voice coming from a throat stuffed with hot gravel. 'You don't look in the least bit like her.' And he stepped back, putting an arm's length of space between them while he still had the strength of mind to do it.

She was a witch. That had to be it. Dora Kavanagh stole men's hearts with a look and kept them her prisoner and they thanked her for it. Richard thought he was the happiest of men and John Gannon knew why. This Pandora might not be all the trouble in the world, but she was the kind of trouble a man with any sense would run from. As for hope — for him there was none.

And Gannon cursed the cracked ribs, the secondary symptoms that promised worse to come, weakening his body to the point that he could no longer run, the weariness that had weakened his spirit to the point that he wasn't sure that he wanted to.

He picked up the pills the doctor had left him. Dora turned away and filled a glass at the sink. He should have been able to take some comfort from the fact that her hands were shaking as much as his. But there was no comfort. And as he swallowed a couple of painkillers he didn't believe that they would help much either. His physical symptoms were just a sideshow, while he had a suspicion that the pain in his heart was terminal.

'John . . . ' He hated it when she said his name like that. Soft, uncertain. Hated it and longed for it. And the longing was worst.

'Don't, Dora.'

'Please, John. I have to tell you something.' He didn't want to hear it. Whatever it was, he didn't want to hear it.

'No.' He turned away and the kitchen

tilted and swayed around him. Dear God, please, he prayed silently. Help me. And as if in answer there was a long, insistent ring at the doorbell. For a moment they remained frozen, unable to move. Then the ring was repeated, and Dora became unstuck from the floor and began to move across the kitchen.

As she passed him, he caught her wrist. 'Promise me something, Dora.'

'Anything,' she said, in a hoarse whisper.

'Promise me that no matter what happens to me you'll take care of Sophie. That you'll make sure she isn't sent back — '

Dora gave a little gasp. This wasn't a man who asked easily for help, yet he was asking for hers, begging for hers. 'I promise.' His golden eyes, brilliant in his drawn face, demanded more. 'I promise I'll look after her, John. I'll keep her safe for you.' And she took his hand from her wrist and silently drew a cross over her heart with the tips of his fingers, before raising them to her lips to kiss them. 'You have my word.'

'Dora . . . ' For long moments he drank in her tender beauty. He knew he shouldn't touch her, that touching her face with just the tip of his finger was every bit as much a betrayal of friendship as taking her to his bed would be, but he couldn't help himself.

His whole body was trembling with his longing for her, his ache to put his arms about her and bury his head in her breast, lose himself in the sweetness of her body. But he had prayed for help and it had come. If he held her now he would be damned for ever.

Dora saw the battle going on inside him, saw the heat clouding his eyes, saw the desire that darkened them and knew they were a reflection of her own longings. Why? John Gannon was a stranger, a man full of secrets. And yet the moment she had switched on the kitchen light at the cottage and startled that oath from him, she had felt that special heart-leap, had heard that inner voice, quiet as a baby's breath, insistent as the drip of a tap. *This one. This is the one. This is the midnight man who comes in your most secret dreams. The man you will remember the day you're dying. Even if you live to be a hundred.* Why else would she have risked so much for him?

Free and clear, and with the evidence of his flight in a stolen plane in front of her, she had not betrayed him. She had gone back to the cottage, faced down the policemen who were waiting for her, and then gone after him to help him. And Sophie.

She raised her hands to cradle his face. His skin was pale, drawn tight across his cheekbones. She wasn't sure which of them was trembling most, all she knew was that she would move heaven and earth to make things right for him.

'John . . . listen to me. I have to tell you something,' she began urgently. 'About Richard and me . . . You've got it all wrong . . . '

The bell rang again, this time accompanied by a determined knocking. 'It's the police, Dora. Go,' he said, pushing her away. 'Before they break the door down.'

'Miss Kavanagh?' There was no need for the warrant card that the man held out for her. She knew that, despite his well-cut suit and silk tie, the man standing before her was indeed a policeman. 'Detective Inspector Reynolds.' And he was not alone. 'PC Johnson,' he said, turning to introduce the young female officer with him. 'May we come in?'

'Do you have a warrant?' she stalled, trying to think.

'I didn't imagine I would need one, Miss Kavanagh. I only want to talk to you.' *That took two of them? What about manpower shortages, cost-cutting?* 'Of course, if you would prefer to come down to the local police station —'

'That won't be necessary, Inspector. I imagine I'm the reason you're here.'

'Mr Gannon?' Gannon was clutching

the kitchen door. 'Mr John Gannon?' He nodded, and the Inspector formally charged him with a number of offences before formally cautioning him. 'If you'll come with me, sir — '

'You can't possibly take him,' Dora said indignantly. 'Surely you can see that he's sick?'

'Leave it, Dora,' he gasped, clutching at his chest as he gave a shallow, painful cough. 'Don't get involved.'

'Damn it, Gannon, I am involved.' She swung back to the policeman. 'You can't take him and throw him in some cell. I won't allow it.'

The constable turned to Gannon and looked at him more carefully. 'He doesn't look too good, guv,' she said. 'Were you hurt landing the plane, Mr Gannon?'

By way of answer, Gannon simply slid down the doorframe and measured his length on the carpet.

'There! What did I tell you?' Dora bent over him, before turning on them. 'You — use that radio thing and get an ambulance here, right now!'

The young woman threw the Inspector a look but didn't argue, unclipping the radio from her collar while Dora cradled Gannon's head in her lap until the ambulance arrived and the paramedics moved her gently away so that they could take his vital signs and attach a drip, prior to loading him onto a stretcher.

'What the devil . . . ?'

Dora looked up to see her brother standing in the open doorway 'Fergus! What on earth are you doing here?'

'I had a call from the Assistant Commissioner. He said you might be in a spot of bother so I thought I'd better come and see what nonsense you've got yourself involved with now — '

'Oh, *Fergus*!' Lost between laughter and tears, she reached out for her brother, hugging him. 'Oh, Fergus. You are a true sight for sore eyes. I honestly can't think of anyone who would be more welcome right now.' She turned to the ambulancemen. 'Where are you taking him?'

They told her the name of the nearest hospital. 'Do you want to come with him, miss?'

Of course she did. She didn't want to let him out of her sight. But she couldn't leave Sophie. Not even with Fergus to babysit. When the little girl woke up and realised that her father wasn't there she would need someone she knew, someone she trusted. 'I can't leave the flat right now, but I'll come as soon as I can. Tell him that, will you? When he comes round.'

'Who is he?' Fergus demanded. Then, 'What's the matter with him?'

'Looks like pneumonia, sir,' one of the paramedics said. 'He'll be back on his feet before you know it.'

'Go with him, Johnson,' the Inspector said, with a jerk of his head. 'Mr Gannon isn't the kind of man to let pneumonia slow him down for long.'

'Why don't you handcuff him to the stretcher?' Dora demanded angrily.

'Dora,' Fergus said, gently, putting his arm about her, heading her in the direction of the sitting room and pouring her a stiff measure of brandy from the tantalus on the sideboard. 'Why don't you tell me what's been going on here?' he said, offering it to her. 'Then we might be able to do something about it.'

'Excuse me, sir, but if you don't mind I have to ask the young lady a few questions first. Is the little girl here, Miss Kavanagh?'

But Fergus intervened. 'And you are?' The Inspector told him. 'Well, Inspector, you'll understand that my sister is in a state of shock. And she won't be answering any questions until her solicitor has arrived. If you'd like to wait downstairs in the lobby, I'm sure the porter will find you a cup of tea.'

'I'm sorry, sir, but I have to know. Is the child here, Miss Kavanagh?'

'She's asleep, Inspector. Please don't disturb her.'

'I'll have to inform the Social Services — '

'No!' Dora's hand flew to her mouth.

'You can't take her away. I promised John I'd look after her.'

'I'm sorry, miss, but — '

Dora realised that emotion was not going to help. 'Sophie's father asked me to take care of her until he was able to do it himself — '

'Father? You'll forgive me, miss, but that's to be proved — '

'Sophie's father,' Dora repeated patiently, 'has just been taken to hospital. I am the only other person in this country that she knows, and if you take her away from me she'll be frightened and quite alone. I promised John Gannon that I would look after her and I will.'

'We will, Inspector,' Fergus said, stepping in. 'In fact, the best thing all round would be for my sister and the child to come back to Marlowe Court with me.' Fergus gave the Inspector his card. 'I think you can take my word that my sister will present herself at the police station with her solicitor first thing in the morning.'

The policeman looked at the card

Fergus had given him. 'It's really not for me to say, sir,' he said, uncomfortably.

'You don't have to.' He lifted the telephone and offered it to the man. 'Call the Assistant Commissioner. I'm sure he'll vouch for me.'

Dora almost felt sorry for the man. It was one thing dealing with a young and slightly distraught woman. Quite another to be faced by Fergus Kavanagh in dictator mode. His sisters might take liberties with his dignity, they might tease him and call him Gussie behind his back when he fussed and worried about them, but to the rest of the world he was the chairman of Kavanagh Industries, and woe betide the rest of the world if they forgot.

'Would you like to see Sophie? Reassure yourself that she's well?'

The man's relief was palpable. 'That would . . . ' He made a gesture that said it all.

Sophie, her rag doll clutched beneath her arm, was sleeping peacefully.

'Thank you, miss. I'll have to let the

Social Services know where she is, of course. I'll leave them to voice any objections they might have directly to Mr Kavanagh.' And for just a moment she thought she saw a hint of amusement in his eyes at the thought.

'How did you find out?' she asked as she escorted the policeman to the door. 'That John was here?'

'Oh. It was the clothes.' Dora frowned. 'You bought the little girl some clothes. You told the constable who questioned you that they were for your niece —'

'My sister's niece.'

'Your sister's niece. Yes. When he made his report, the station sergeant knew you were lying because his wife was at the same antenatal class as Mrs Shelton, which meant your, er, sister's niece could only be six or seven months old. The clothes you'd bought were for a much older child.'

Dora grinned wryly. 'I wouldn't make a very successful criminal, would I?'

'I do hope not, miss.'

The following morning Fergus instructed his chauffeur to take a detour via the hospital on their way back to Marlowe Court, so that Dora and Sophie could see Gannon. She'd phoned earlier and been told that he had had 'a comfortable night', but nothing more. She was directed to the appropriate ward, but, unable to see him, she enquired at the ward sister's desk.

'I'm looking for John Gannon. He was brought in last night,' she said, picking up Sophie, who was fidgeting nervously at her knees.

'And you are?'

'Dora Kavanagh. This is Sophie, his daughter.'

'I'm sorry, Miss Kavanagh, but Mr Gannon has expressed a wish not to receive any visitors.'

Dora stared at the girl for a moment, then she frowned. 'I'm sorry?'

'He doesn't want visitors.'

'But . . . I don't understand. This is

his daughter . . . he must want to see her.' The nurse looked sympathetic, but she was immovable.

'I'm sorry.'

Dora could not get her head around what the woman was saying, looking about her as if Gannon might somehow just appear, look at her with that lazy smile. But he didn't.

She didn't understand. And then she thought perhaps she did. He thought that she had betrayed him. That while he was sleeping she had called the police. She could understand that he would be angry, that he would refuse to see her. But to refuse to see Sophie?

Sophie began to grizzle, and Dora cuddled her, comforting her. Maybe he thought she would be frightened by the hospital. Maybe he was right about that, if nothing else.

'How is he?' she asked helplessly.

'He had a comfortable night. The doctor will be seeing him again later.'

Dora wanted to grab her by the apron front and shake her, tell her that she *had* to see him because she loved him . . . that she had to tell him . . . But the woman was simply doing what Gannon had told her to do. 'Can I write to him? Or has he forbidden that, too?'

The nurse gave her something close to a smile. 'Not as far as I know. Do you want to write something now?'

'Yes.' Then, 'No.' She needed to sit down and explain everything properly, not dash off a few words on a scrap of paper. Or maybe that would do it. 'Actually . . . ' The nurse pushed a pen and a piece of paper across the desk, and without even stopping to think she wrote simply — 'Sophie is safe. I love you, Dora.' Then she added Fergus's telephone number before folding the paper and handing it to the nurse.

'I'll see he gets it,' she said.

'Thank you.' With one last glance about her, in the desperate hope that she might catch a glimpse of him through some open doorway, so that even if he wouldn't see her she could see him, Dora acknowledged defeat and left the hospital.

She could scarcely contain her impatience until they arrived at Marlowe Court — the house where she was born, the house where Fergus lived these days in lonely state, with just his staff for company — certain that John would have called her to say that he understood, to ask her to come back because he needed her. He hadn't. He didn't.

Fergus had a call from Gannon's solicitor, arranging for Sophie to remain in his guardianship while the results of the blood tests were awaited. 'Why you?' she demanded jealously. 'He doesn't know you. He's never met you.'

'He's protecting you, Dora. He's only too aware that he involved you in all kinds of trouble. I don't think you realise quite how much.' And with that she had to be satisfied. That and writing a long letter explaining everything. About Richard, and that he was married to her sister. Explaining why she hadn't told him the truth. Explaining how the police had tracked him down.

It was returned, unopened, three endless days later. And her headlong rush back to London, determined to lay siege to the hospital until they let her see him and hang the consequences, proved futile. He had discharged himself and she had no idea where to find him. His solicitor, however, did not seem surprised to see her. But he too had had his orders and was unable to help.

Dora was standing outside his offices, taxing her brain, refusing to admit defeat, certain there must be something she had overlooked, when the receptionist who had made her a cup of coffee while she had waited to be seen — a young woman who had read about and shown enormous interest in her aid convoys — appeared at her elbow. 'Have you ever been to the local magistrates' court, Miss Kavanagh?' she asked.

Dora frowned. 'Magistrates' court?'

'I'm sure you'd find it interesting. Next Friday, for instance. At about ten o'clock.' And with that she was gone.

* * *

Dora spent the following week amusing Sophie, talking to her all the time, so that the child's understanding of English expanded at an almost unbelievable rate.

She took her shopping, delighting in buying her clothes and simple toys, and as the weather settled back into the hot, still days of perfect August weather she began to teach her to swim in Fergus's swimming pool.

But all the time the thought of Friday haunted her with the promise of seeing John, with the threat that he might really never want to see her again.

Well, he would have to. She would make him. And she would make him listen to her. She loved him. 'Swim, Dora! Sophie swim!' Sophie came running up with her armbands to be blown up. She loved Sophie, too, and she swept her up into her lap and began to tickle her until the child screamed with laughter. They were making so much noise that they didn't hear the footsteps behind them.

'What's all this, then?'

'Poppy, Richard!' Dora scooped Sophie up in one arm, hugging her sister and brother-in-law with the other. 'How lovely to see you. When did you get back?'

'Last night. Hi, kitten,' Poppy said, gently rubbing the child's cheek. 'I understand you've been having interesting times.'

Dora pulled a face. 'You've been talking to Fergus.'

'Mmm. Anything we can do?'

'Drive me to London tomorrow?' she asked. 'I haven't got a car here and I've got a date at a magistrates' court. I was going to hire a car, but to be honest I'm scared to death — '

'What about Fergus? I thought he was handling everything?'

Her brother couldn't have taken over more effectively if it had been a business coup. And he was determined that she keep out of it. 'He is. But do you know, Poppy, he's somehow quite forgotten to mention that John is in court tomorrow? Why is that, do you think?'

'Have you asked him?'

'No. I haven't told him I know about it. If I did he'd move heaven and earth to keep me from going.'

'He's just being protective, Dora. You know what the press are like . . . you went down to the cottage to escape them . . . '

'I don't give a hang about the press or anyone else. I'm going, whether you come or not,' she said, with grim determination.

'Hey, I didn't say I wouldn't. But . . . well, actually, I can't. I've got a meeting that I simply can't cancel — it's the reason we've flown back from the States early. But we'll drive you up to town. You can drop me off and

Richard will go to court with you — won't you, sweetheart?'

'No problem,' he said. 'But what about this little charmer?'

'Mrs Harris will look after her. They're great friends.'

Poppy laughed. 'I'll bet. Mrs Harris is a frustrated mother hen. She must be in her element with this little one to fuss over. Will she come to me, do you think?'

'Give her a little while to get used to you. We're just going in the pool — why don't you join us?' Poppy gave the water a doubtful look. 'It's all right, Fergus has turned the heating up for Sophie.'

'Wow. He must be smitten too. I'll go and change.' She disappeared towards the changing rooms in a glamorous swirl of cream and peach silk.

'How's John?' Richard asked.

'Out of hospital. Apart from that I know nothing. He . . . ' She couldn't say it. She couldn't say, He won't see me. 'He's keeping his distance. Because

261

of the court case.'

He must have sensed her uncertainty, because he said, 'But he left his daughter with you.'

'With Fergus, technically.' Richard raised his eyebrows and she smiled. 'The Social Services wanted to whisk her away and put her into a foster home until the paternity thing has been settled, but you know Fergus. He threw his weight about a bit. Called some friends. Came up trumps.'

'And John has a hearing at the magistrates' court tomorrow?'

She nodded. 'I'm scared, Richard. Really scared. He said they would have to make an example of him. To stop other people . . . ' And suddenly she was shaking so much that she had to put Sophie down. 'Suppose they send him to prison?'

'You'll cope. You're both strong enough to handle it.' He gave her a hug. 'Hey, come on. Don't let the little one see you cry. What's her name?'

Dora sniffed. 'Sophie.'

'She's amazingly like John, you know.'

'Really?' Dora laughed through her tears.

'When he was a kid. Solemn and bony. What happened to her mother? Do you know?'

'Only that she died.'

All the doubts were there in her voice. She still couldn't quite shake them. 'He's okay, you know, Dora. A good man.'

'Is he?' Yet how could she have ever doubted him? He had risked everything for Sophie. If only she could have trusted him completely, he would be here with her now — with her and Sophie.

Richard nodded, as if her question had been purely rhetorical, not requiring an answer, then he crouched down and held out his hand. 'How d'you do, Sophie? I'm Richard. I know your daddy.' Sophie regarded him for a moment, then handed him her armbands. Richard laughed and instantly obeyed this mute command to inflate them.

★ ★ ★

The magistrates' court was unbelievably busy. Dark-suited solicitors, bewigged barristers, witnesses waiting to give evidence, anxious family members. Dora and Richard squeezed in at the back of the hot, crowded gallery and he took her hand as she grew increasingly nervous. 'Are you going to be all right, Dora?'

'What? Oh, yes.' And then he was there, in the dock. 'Oh, John,' she whispered, grasping Richard's hand tighter. 'Oh, my poor darling.' He looked gaunt, exhausted, far worse than she had expected. The only colour in his skin was the faded tan that gave him a sickly yellow look, and his eyes and cheeks had dark shadows. Even the cleft in his chin seemed deeper, more noticeable. 'He looks so ill,' she said, half rising. The movement caught Gannon's attention and he glanced up.

For a moment he stared at her. Then quite deliberately he looked away again, facing directly in front of him as the magistrate began to speak.

'John Gannon, you have pleaded guilty to the charges made against you — '

'When?' Dora demanded, surprised. 'When did he do that?'

Richard glanced at her. 'Last week. Surely — ' The magistrate glanced up at the gallery, waiting impatiently for silence. When he had it, he continued.

'I've received an impressive number of reports as to your good character, and the mitigating circumstances in this case, but I have to say, Mr Gannon, that in your desperation to recover your daughter from a refugee camp you have shown an almost reckless disregard for the law . . . ' The man droned on, listing, it seemed to an anguished Dora, every possible misdemeanour that John Gannon might have committed since he had left his pram. 'Taking all this into account, I have no option but to sentence you to six months — '

'No!' Dora cried out, leaping to her feet before Richard could restrain her. 'No!' The cry tore out from the suffocatingly hot little gallery into the court-room, and seemed to swell and hang there while everyone turned and stared at her.

'Six months,' the magistrate repeated, glaring at Dora, daring her to say another word. But she was beyond words. As the blood seeped from her head Dora Kavanagh crumpled in a heap against her brother-in-law and knew no more, until the ornate moulding on the ceiling of the clerk's office, gradually swam into focus.

For a moment she couldn't think where she was, what had happened. Then, as the horror of it came back in a rush, she tried to sit up. 'I've got to see him,' she said, glaring at the stranger whose firm hand was restraining her. 'John Gannon,' she said urgently. 'I've got to see him. Now.'

'I'm afraid you can't, miss. He's already gone.'

10

Dora stared at the man, one of the court ushers, her head still swimming. 'Gone?' she asked stupidly, her limbs like water as she struggled to sit up for a moment longer and then gave in, subsiding back onto the sofa. It seemed an unlikely item of furniture for a court usher's office. But maybe they had to deal with a lot of this kind of thing.

'You just lie still, miss,' the man said as she fell back. 'You'll feel better in a moment.' It sounded like the voice of experience, but she still doubted it.

How on earth could she ever feel better until she'd seen John, made him listen to her? She'd been so sure that today she would have the chance to confront him, make him hear her out. Instead it had all gone horribly wrong. She'd fainted. *Fainted!* Who had ever heard of anything so pathetic . . . ?

She closed her eyes against the fierce sunlight streaming in through the windows and tried to concentrate over the throbbing of her head. John had gone, the man had said. Where? Had he been put in handcuffs, whisked away in one of those barred vans that she had seen on the news to serve his sentence? Surely they couldn't have done that to him? He hadn't hurt anyone . . .

'Gone?' she repeated. 'You did say he had — '

'That's right, miss,' the man repeated patiently. 'Now, you just stay there until your friend comes back with his car,' he added warningly, as she made another attempt to sit up.

'So soon . . . '

'They don't hang about once the case has been heard,' he assured her. 'Now, do you want to try that again? Slowly, mind.' Quite suddenly there didn't seem to be any rush — actually, there didn't seem to be much point in moving at all — but Dora allowed herself to be eased up into a sitting position. 'Just you have a sip of this, then sit there quietly for a minute. You'll be right as ninepence in no time.'

Dora drank a little of the water she was offered and remembered her manners. 'Thank you. I'm sorry to be such a nuisance.' She turned as the door opened. 'Richard! He's gone . . . '

'I know. I tried to speak to him but I was too late. Look, can you move? I've got the car outside with a traffic warden watching it, but she said no more than two minutes . . . '

'Of course I can move.' She lurched to her feet, and Richard took her arm as she swayed and put her hand to her head.

'She needs to take her time,' the usher warned. 'Until she's quite recovered.'

'I have to speak to him. It's absolutely essential. He thinks I called the police, but I didn't . . . You'll have to see him — tell him.'

'You can tell him yourself, Dora.'

'But I can't . . . don't you see? He

won't speak to me.'

Richard stared at her. 'But I thought ... Oh, good grief, you moved too soon ... ' As the colour drained from her face once more, Richard picked her up and carried her out, easing her onto the back seat of the car, where she sat groggily while he fastened the seat belt.

'Will you be all right, sir?' the usher enquired doubtfully, bringing up the rear with her handbag.

'I'm just going to pick up my wife. Her sister,' he explained. 'She'll look after Dora. Thanks for your help back there.'

The drive home passed in a blur of misery. Dora was vaguely aware of Poppy getting into the car, sitting in the back with her, putting her arm around her. But she was beyond comfort. She had thought that when John saw her everything would be all right.

What a fool she'd been. He had stared at her as if she wasn't there. Cut her dead. And it would be six months before she could see him, because he'd never let her visit him in prison. She didn't need to ask, it had been there in his face.

But surely he would want to know about Sophie? How she was? What she was doing? Photographs . . . As quickly as hope flared it died. Fergus would take care of that. That was why Fergus had been given responsibility for her. Not because of his influence, or because no one would dare challenge his authority. John Gannon had asked Fergus to help him because he couldn't bear to have anything to do with a woman who would betray him. And Fergus had agreed, hoping to keep them apart. There was no point in appealing to her brother for help because he didn't approve of John. He hadn't said as much, but it was as clear as day that he didn't believe John Gannon was the right man for his precious little sister.

Oh, he'd done everything for Sophie and dealt with all the paperwork once the blood tests had proved without doubt that she was John's daughter. But, as he never ceased to remind her, John Gannon had come close to involving her in a court case, and she could easily have been standing in the dock beside him. As if she would have cared.

The trouble with Fergus was that he'd never been in love, so he couldn't be expected to understand.

'Come on, darling, we're home,' Poppy said, when they reached Marlowe Court. 'Why don't you go upstairs and lie down for a while? You still look pretty shaky.'

'No, I've got to see Sophie. Where's Sophie?' The child was her only link with John, and she had a sudden morbid fear that Fergus would whisk her away somewhere. 'I must see Sophie,' she repeated.

'Hey, calm down, love. She'll be in the kitchen with Mrs Harris, I expect. Come on, we'll go and find her.' But Dora was yards ahead of her.

Sophie, wrapped in a huge apron,

was sitting at the work-counter sticking currant eyes and buttons onto a trayful of gingerbread men, but she slipped down from the chair and ran to Dora as soon as she saw her, flinging her arms about her knees. Dora bent and hugged her. Too tightly. She mustn't cling to the child. She would have another life, somewhere else, with John. She loosened her grip and looked at his little girl. There was such a change in her after just a few days of Mrs Harris's good cooking.

'You'll save me one of those, won't you darling?' she said, a little shakily, her throat tight with tears she could not shed as she helped the child back up onto the chair.

Poppy took her arm. 'Go on now, Dora. Lie down for a while. Mrs Harris and I will look after Sophie. Maybe have a swim later.'

She begrudged every minute that she would lose of Sophie's company, knew she should be thinking, not resting, but her head was aching so much. 'Perhaps you're right,' she said. 'Just for half an hour . . . '

'Take as long as you need, she'll be fine with us. Go. We'll see you at dinner.'

The thought of food made Dora feel faint. All week the thought of food had made her feel faint. Maybe that was why, in the end, she had fainted. It wouldn't do. She'd need all her strength if she was going to get through this. 'I just need an hour.'

'Take all the time you need.'

★ ★ ★

Fergus arrived home just after four. 'Where's Dora?' he asked, as he walked down to the poolside.

Poppy, standing beside the pool in a sleek white one-piece bathing suit, waiting for Richard to change and join her, turned at the sound of her brother's voice. 'She's lying down. She had a bit of a wobbly turn.'

'Why?' Fergus asked sharply. 'What's

the matter with her?'

Belatedly remembering that Fergus wasn't supposed to know about her sister's trip into London, she said, 'Nothing. It's just the heat.'

'It's probably just as well. I've got Gannon in the car; he's come to collect his daughter.' He looked about him. 'Where is Sophie?'

'In the kitchen with Mrs Harris. She's just started tea, so you'd better ask Mr Gannon in for a drink while he's waiting.'

'You're sure Dora is resting?'

'She was fast asleep when I looked in on her about ten minutes ago. Why, Fergus? Are you trying keeping them apart?'

Fergus pulled a face. 'I know better than to try and keep Dora from anything she wants, Poppy. It's Gannon who doesn't want to see her. He just wants to collect his little girl and go.'

'That's pretty shabby, considering all she's done for him.'

'Maybe it is, and I won't deny that

I'll miss Sophie about the place, but he's adamant.'

'Oh, Fergus!'

'Don't 'Oh, Fergus!' me, Poppy. This is entirely his decision.'

'But one you have done nothing to alter?'

'I've seen him; you haven't. The man's mind is made up. But, since Dora is out of the way, I'll tell him to come in and wait for Sophie. You can give him a drink if you want to. It'll give you the chance to tell him exactly what you think of him while I go and check on progress in the kitchen.' With that he turned and walked quickly back to the front of the house.

'Did I hear your brother?' Richard asked, crossing the pool terrace from the changing room.

'You did.'

'Pity. I was rather hoping we might have the pool to ourselves for a while.'

'There's no one here now,' she pointed out, smiling seductively at him, then giving a little scream of delight as

Richard grabbed her and swept her off her feet. Then she kissed him.

John Gannon, rounding the corner of the house, stopped abruptly. Fergus Kavanagh had told him that Dora was asleep or he would never have got out of the car. Not that Kavanagh had needed much convincing that it would be wiser for them not to meet. He was clearly not about to encourage a man who had so nearly got his sister into serious trouble with the law. And into serious trouble with her marriage — although whether he knew that or was simply guessing he couldn't be sure. But Gannon didn't blame him for wanting him in and out of his house with all possible haste. A clean cut. Painful, but necessary.

And it had been painful. It had been like cutting out his own heart, lying in a hospital side ward, hearing her plead with the nurse. To hold her letter in his hand and not open it. To tell his solicitor that under no circumstances must she be given his address. But it had been right. He had known it. He hadn't needed Fergus Kavanagh to look at him as if he was trouble. He was.

But even then, somewhere deep in the recesses of his soul, he had still hoped. Until today, when he had turned and seen her in the public gallery with Richard. And then she had cried out, and he knew he couldn't face Richard either. Because everything he was feeling would surely show. He wouldn't be able to hide his guilt, or his pain.

And now his worst nightmare was before him. She was there, wrapped in the arms of his oldest friend. A man who was her husband. A man who loved her. He could understand that, because he loved her himself. He loved her beyond reason. If he had ever doubted it, he knew it now. Just as he knew that he should have trusted his own instincts and stayed in the car.

Now the breath was being squeezed from his body, and he grabbed at his tie to loosen it as he fought the suffocating jealousy, spinning round to make good his escape before they saw him.

'John!' Too late. He stopped, slowly turned as Richard came towards him, hand outstretched, grinning broadly. 'Damn, but it's good to see you. And Dora's been quite frantic.' He turned and held out his hand to the woman behind him. 'John's here at last, darling.'

Gannon forced himself to stand there, to take Richard's hand. To let nothing of his feelings show as he turned to her, to smile as if his world wasn't ending.

'Richard — ' he began, then stopped, confused. The woman behind Richard was not Dora. The woman Richard had been kissing was not Dora.

'I told you I was the happiest man in the world,' he was saying. 'Now you can see why.' He half turned. 'Poppy, darling, this is John Gannon. You remember? I wanted him for our best man but he was away in some far-flung corner of a foreign field. Where *were* you at Christmas, John?'

'Rwanda,' he replied. 'I think.'

She was like Dora superficially. She had the same long fair hair, the same slender body. But she was taller, older, oozed the kind of glamour that goes with the world of fashion and beauty. 'Poppy?' He repeated her name as if it was somehow imbued with magic.

'Dora's big sister,' she confirmed. 'He still couldn't take it in. Poppae and Pandora,' she added helpfully, mistaking his confusion. 'Mother was into all that ancient stuff.'

He swallowed, trying to get his head round this. 'Er . . . how come Fergus escaped?'

Poppy laughed. 'Family legend has it that Mother wanted to call him Perseus, but Father put his foot down. Said everyone would call him Percy.'

He was still looking from one of them to the other. 'And you're married to Richard?'

'If he's told you any different, he's lying,' she said, with a grin. 'And he'll have to pay a forfeit.' She started to pull her husband back towards the pool.

'Where's Dora?' he demanded, his urgency stopping her at the edge of the water, 'I have to see her.'

'But I thought — ' Then, 'Dora's upstairs, John, lying down. She fainted in court. It was all a bit much for her — the heat and everything. But you know that; you were there.'

'Where can I find her?' he insisted. 'I have to see her now.'

Dora's big sister smiled. 'Top of the stairs, third door on the right.' And with that the pair of them disappeared in a splash.

* * *

Gannon walked slowly up the broad oak staircase. Dora wasn't married to Richard. He kept saying it over and over in his head, and still he didn't quite dare to believe it. He could see how the confusion had happened. The policeman had assumed she was Poppy and called her Mrs Marriott, and he had accepted it without question. But why had she let him go on thinking it?

The third door on the right. He tapped lightly but there was no answer, In the silence he heard a burst of childish laughter from the kitchen. Sophie. He had found Sophie. He had brought her home safe through all kinds of dangers. He would not be stopped now by something as mundane as a door. He grasped the handle and opened it, and after that nothing mattered. Only that he loved her.

She was asleep. Her hair spread out across the pillow, her golden limbs lightly covered with a sheet. Sleeping Beauty. He longed to wake her with a kiss, but this wasn't a fairy tale and he was no prince.

Instead he knelt beside the bed, propping his chin upon his hands, every part of him aching for her to wake so that he could take her in his arms, yet reluctant to lose this moment of perfect hope. The promise had been there in her name. He should never have lost hope.

And then he realised something extraordinary. Her cheek was wet. He reached out and touched her skin with the tip of his finger, carried the salt taste of her tears to his lips. She had been crying in her sleep.

'Dora.' He said her name softly. Then, 'Dora, my darling girl.'

Dora stirred, opened her eyes. She thought she'd heard John call her name, and for a moment could not decide whether she was asleep or awake. Then as her eyes focused on his face she knew that she had to be dreaming. John was locked up, unattainable . . . Yet could dreams be this real?

She didn't dare to put her hand, try to touch him, afraid his beloved image would simply disappear. Instead she said his name.

'John?' she whispered.

'Yes, my darling.'

He'd called her his darling. She'd felt

his breath against her cheek as he said the world and still she didn't quite dare to believe it. She stretched out her hand to touch his as it lay on the sheet beside her, then snatched it back again, terribly afraid that he was simply a figment of her desperate longing, that if she tried to hold him she would wake up and the emptiness would rush back.

'Why did you pretend, Dora?' he asked.

He spoke again. Could she answer? Only with the truth. 'Because I was afraid.'

'Of me?'

'No!' She reached out then and grasped his hand, desperate to convince him. 'Of myself. Of my feelings.' And then she knew. 'I'm not dreaming, am I?' He shook his head, took her hand and placed it against his cheek, kissed her fingers, her palm, with such sweetness . . . 'But I don't understand. I heard the magistrate sentence you . . . ' She sat up abruptly, suddenly wide awake. 'Oh, my God, you've escaped — '

'No!' He put his finger to her lips to stop her. 'No, darling.' And he rose to sit on the edge of the bed, touching her face, her hair, before pulling her against his chest, holding her there. 'I'll never escape — don't you know that? The six months the magistrate gave me was suspended, but I'm a prisoner still. Your prisoner. For life.' He produced a scrap of paper from his shirt pocket and offered it to her. It was the note she'd scribbled in the hospital. 'Did you mean it?'

She lifted her head and looked him full in the eyes. 'You know I did. Why wouldn't you see me, John? Why did you send back my letter?'

'You know why.' She shook her head. 'Dora, I thought you were married to Richard — '

'But surely Fergus — someone — must have explained — ' She gave a little gasp. 'But why would they? No one else knew. Oh, John, if only I'd had the courage to trust you completely.'

It was his turn to look confused. 'You

had courage enough for ten, Dora. I don't understand. If you didn't think Richard was keeping us apart why *did* you think I was staying away from you?'

She coloured. 'I've been such an idiot . . . ' Her doubts seemed so small, so petty now.

'Hey, come on.' He held her close for a moment. 'It can't possibly be that bad.'

'But it is. I thought . . . ' There really was no easy way to say it. 'I thought you didn't want to see me because of the police.'

'The police? What on earth have they to do with this?'

'You were asleep. I could have called them. You thought I might. It was why you didn't let me go to the corner shop.'

'Ah. Yes. I see.'

'You were right, actually. Though I wasn't going to call the police. Just Fergus. I thought he could help you.'

'But you didn't. Even when I was asleep.'

'Are you so sure?'

'The police explained how they found me, about the clothes.'

'I'm so sorry.'

'Don't keep saying that.' He drew back, put a little distance between them. 'You've nothing to be sorry for. I'm the one with all the apologies to make, all the questions to answer.'

Dora kneeled up on the bed and put her arms about his neck. 'No, John. No doubts. No questions. You're here now. Nothing else matters.'

'Not even Sophie's mother?' He looked down at her. 'You haven't asked about her.'

'You'll tell me if you want to. But you don't have to — '

'You've a right to know.'

He took her arms from around his neck and for a moment held her hands. Then he let them go, stood up and walked to the window, staring out across the dusty late-summer country-side. She didn't protest. He had something to get off his chest, and she was happy to listen if it made him feel better. But she'd learned her lesson about being begrudging with her trust. She knew now that honour was something so natural to him that he would never hurt anyone intentionally, even if it meant his own pain.

She slipped from the bed, pulled on a wrap and curled up on the window seat beneath him, her arms about her knees, waiting patiently for him to unburden himself.

'We were in a cellar,' he said finally. 'Just Elena and me. It was chance. We'd never met before, but we'd both run for the same cover when a sniper opened up. I shouldn't even have been there, but my car had broken down and I'd been trying to get someone to fix it . . . ' He paused. 'Normally a sniper doesn't hang about for long; he's too easy to pinpoint, too vulnerable. I thought we'd be there an hour or two at the most, but then as night fell the bombardment opened up and we were trapped. It was cold, and there was nothing to burn for heat, but we shared what little food we had. I had some chocolate, some water. She had some bread. She'd been shopping for bread . . .'

'Come and sit down, John.' Dora patted the cushioned seat beside her and he turned away from the window. She smiled up at him.

'Don't!' He subsided onto the seat beside her, leaning forward to cover her lovely mouth with his hand. 'Don't smile at me. Not until you've heard it all.' And only when he was sure that she would obey him did he take his hand away.

'Tell me, then,' she encouraged. 'Tell me about Elena. What happened?' She asked only because he needed to tell her, not because she needed to be told. It was all so obvious. Two people alone in a freezing dark cellar, afraid that any moment a shell would land on top of them, that they were going to die, and offering each other the only comfort they could. He told his story and it was much as she had expected.

Dora wanted to ask if Elena had been young, pretty. But she resisted the little tug of jealousy. She knew it didn't matter. What had happened hadn't been about desire, or love. It had been about need.

'And then it was over and we were still alive. I had a story to file and she had a family to find, somewhere, if they had survived. We were both in a hurry to be somewhere else, and what had happened . . . it was just something that happens during a war. But I scribbled my address on a piece of paper and gave it to her. Perhaps even then I had an idea that she might need it.'

'Would you have married her, John?'

'I would have looked after her. I'm going to marry you.'

'Are you?' The statement certainly had a deliciously determined ring to it. 'But when? There's still so much to do. So many more people to help.'

'No more aid convoys, Dora,' he said urgently. 'You can't go back.'

'Because of Sophie? What you did?'

'Because of Sophie,' he confirmed. 'And because I love you, Dora.' He laid his palm against her cheek. 'Because I cannot live without you.'

'But there are so many other children just like Sophie.' She looked up at him, willing him to understand that she couldn't simply walk away. 'I can't let them down. They need me.'

'They will have both of us. I've already been approached about a book and possibly a television documentary.'

'But that's wonderful!'

'I'm glad you approve. But it will take time, and together we could raise a lot of money now.'

'Together?'

'You and me and Sophie . . . '

'We could organise some kind of appeal to help women like Elena and their children,' she said. 'Name it after her, perhaps.'

'Or Sophie.'

'Or Sophie,' she agreed.

'So, Dora. Do I have to go down on my knees for an answer?' Then, as she began to remove the links from his cuffs, 'What are you doing?'

'You asked me to marry you, John,' she said, as she slipped the knot of his tie and began to unfasten his shirt buttons. 'I'm a great believer in actions speaking louder than words. In showing, not telling.'

'Like driving a lorry into a war zone instead of standing about and wringing your hands?'

She regarded him with a small smile. 'I knew you'd understand.'

'I'm definitely getting the hang of it,' he said, and pulled the tie of her silk wrapper so that it fell open. 'So, what did you have in mind?' he asked, his golden eyes dark with something much more dangerous than simple curiosity.

'This,' she said, pushing aside his shirt, running her hands lightly over his chest. 'I've been thinking about nothing else for days. And this.'

She leaned into him to kiss the deep hollow at the base of his neck, trailing warm kisses over his throat, across his shoulder, nipping at his skin with small, even teeth, delighting in the agonised groan she drew from somewhere deep inside him.

Then she tilted her head back and looked at him through lowered lashes, her lips parted provocatively. 'Feel free to join in any time you like,' she invited. 'This is a game for two.'

'This is no game, Dora,' he said, sweeping aside her wrapper to slide his hands about her waist, draw her into the warmth of his body, at last free to let her know how much he wanted her, needed her. 'This is as serious as it gets. I love you. I think I loved you the moment I first saw you, standing there with Sophie in your arms, so *indignant* that anyone would have the nerve to break in.'

Her eyes widened. 'It wasn't that. I was just indignant that you would bring a child along with you on your house-breaking sorties . . . ' She stared at him. 'But even then I knew you were different, that you were my midnight man, my lover coming to me in the silence of the night. You're right, John. This *is* serious. Kiss me, my love. Hold me. Love me and promise me that you won't ever stop.'

John Gannon promised. And promised. And promised.

★ ★ ★

'Daddee!' Sophie, splashing in the pool, saw her father walking across the terrace and slithered away from Richard, splashing energetically to the steps where he reached down and scooped her up, holding her close, not caring about the fact that she was dripping wet. 'I can swim,' she said.

'So I can see,' he said, laughing, taking the towel Poppy handed him and wrapping it around her, drying her face. 'Who's been teaching you all this good stuff?'

'Sophie and Gussie.'

'Gussie?'

'I think she's referring to me,' Fergus

said, carrying out a tray of glasses and a bottle of champagne. 'She's picked it up from the girls, I suppose. They think I don't know . . . Where's Dora?'

'She'll be down in a minute.' John Gannon saw the challenge in Fergus Kavanagh's eyes and met it head on before nodding towards the champagne. 'Are you just glad that I'm staying for dinner, or is the champagne to celebrate something in particular?'

'The length of time you've been upstairs, it had better be something in particular, don't you think?' Fergus enquired as he loosened the wire.

'Will a wedding do?'

Fergus paused to regard him levelly. 'A wedding? Isn't that rather sudden? Couldn't we just have an engagement to be getting along with. A very long engagement.'

'Frankly, Fergus, this has already been the longest week of my entire life. But you'll have to fight it out with Dora, she seems to be rather keen to get things moving.'

Perhaps it was fortunate that the champagne cork chose that moment to burst from the bottle, avoiding the need for an answer.

'Fergus!' They both turned as Dora walked out onto the terrace behind them. She went up to her brother, put her arms about him and kissed him. 'You're a darling. Thank you for bringing John home safe. I was sure you didn't approve, but how could I ever have doubted you?'

Fergus cleared his throat. 'Sophie's here,' he said. 'You're here. Where else would he go?' But for a small still moment, in the excitement, he regarded John Gannon with a look that warned him never to do anything to hurt his sister. The answer he saw in the other man's face must have reassured him, because quite suddenly he grinned and began spilling the champagne into the glasses. 'Come on, everyone, you heard the man. This is a celebration.'

'What's a silly . . . a silly . . . bashun, Gussie?' Sophie asked.

Poppy and Dora were unable to look at one another. Richard coughed. No one, but no one, ever called Fergus Kavanagh Gussie to his face. 'Celebration, poppet. Celebration. We celebrate when something special happens.' He took the child from John. 'Grown-ups do it with a drink called champagne. Little tots like you drink . . . milk.'

'Spoilsport,' Poppy muttered.

'Strawberry milk,' Fergus elaborated. 'Or maybe banana milk. With a chocolate biscuit. Come on, we'll go and ask Mrs Harris if she's got some for you.'

'You know, I think it's time Gussie got married,' Dora said as he disappeared through the French windows, and gave her sister a long look through narrowed eyes, 'before he settles into the role of universal uncle.'

'Or, worse, starts to breed cats,' Poppy said, rather too quickly, her hands suddenly protective of her waist.

'I don't think there's any danger of cats,' Dora replied thoughtfully. 'Besides, he's allergic to them. So it'll have to be marriage. I can't think why we haven't thought of it before.'

'Surely he's capable of thinking it for himself,' John murmured.

Dora linked her arm in his. 'Poor Fergus has been so busy looking after us all his life, and doing his best to keep us out of trouble, that he's never had the time to look for a suitable wife. He's not the kind of man to stumble across one in a thunderstorm, you see, he's far too well-organised for that — and what kind of girl would have the temerity to break in to Marlowe Court?'

'Perhaps you two should get together and set about finding one for him,' Richard suggested. 'After all, once you've found the right girl it won't take any time at all.'

'Won't it? Why not?' John asked.

Richard grinned. 'You mean Dora hasn't told you? Love at first sight is a Kavanagh thing. Once they home in on you there's no escape. And you know what else has just occurred to me?'

Dora, John and Poppy waited while he replenished their glasses.

'Well?' Poppy demanded.

'Nothing much. Except that they say everything comes in threes. And I don't see any reason why that shouldn't include weddings. Do you?' He raised his glass. 'What shall we drink to?'

'Weddings in general?' Poppy offered.

'Our wedding in particular,' suggested John.

'Weddings all round,' Dora concluded, smiling at the man she loved. 'And the sooner the better.'

THE END

We do hope that you have enjoyed reading this large print book.

Did you know that all of our titles are available for purchase?

We publish a wide range of high quality large print books including:
Romances, Mysteries, Classics
General Fiction
Non Fiction and Westerns

Special interest titles available in large print are:
The Little Oxford Dictionary
Music Book, Song Book
Hymn Book, Service Book

Also available from us courtesy of Oxford University Press:
Young Readers' Dictionary
(large print edition)
Young Readers' Thesaurus
(large print edition)

For further information or a free brochure, please contact us at:
Ulverscroft Large Print Books Ltd.,
The Green, Bradgate Road, Anstey,
Leicester, LE7 7FU, England.
Tel: (00 44) **0116 236 4325**
Fax: (00 44) **0116 234 0205**

Other titles in the
Linford Romance Library:

A HEART DIVIDED

Sheila Holroyd

Life is hard for Anne and her father under Cromwell's harsh rule, which has reduced them from wealth to poverty. When tragedy strikes it looks as if there is no one she can turn to for help. With one friend fearing for his life and another apparently lost to her, a man she hates sees her as a way of fulfilling all his ambitions. Will she have to surrender to him or lose everything?

SAFE HARBOUR

Cara Cooper

When Adam Hawthorne with his sharp suit and devastating looks drives into the town of Seaport, Cassandra knows he's dangerous. Not only do his plans threaten to ruin her successful harbourside restaurant, but also Adam stirs painful memories she'd rather forget. When Cassandra's sister Ellie turns up, in trouble as usual, Cassandra needs all her considerable strength to cope. But will discovering dark secrets from Adam's past change Cassandra's future? And will he be her saviour or her downfall?

THE HAPPY HOSTAGE

Charles Stuart

When an agreement is made with the U.S.A. to build missile bases in Carmania, Elisabeth Renner and her friends plot to kidnap the American ambassador to Carmania and force the agreement to be cancelled. However, they get the wrong man: Charles Gresham, a budding British business tycoon. And he soon finds himself sympathising with his pretty captor. Then Elisabeth reluctantly decides to call it all off, and things really go wrong — when Charles doesn't want to be released!

STILL THE ONE

Joan Reeves

Ally Fletcher fights her way through a torrential downpour to Mr Burke Winslow and his bride at their marriage ceremony! Ally's arrival at the church halts the nuptials when she delivers her bombshell: the groom is already married — to her! However, this businessman isn't in love: he needs a wife for two weeks, purely for financial reasons. Anyone will do — even his insufferable ex. Soon Burke and Ally are temporarily reliving their disastrous marriage — and their sensational, sizzling honeymoon . . .

LESSONS IN LOVE

Chrissie Loveday

1963. Lucy's first teaching job turns out to be more than she bargained for . . . fired with enthusiasm to show her teaching skills, she is brought down to earth when she faces a depressing room and difficult pupils. However, her mum is always there for her and she soon begins to find herself with an increasingly complicated love life. Who should she choose to spend time with? And why is the Headmaster so concerned about the company she keeps?

SEA OF LOVE

Roberta Grieve

When she is left destitute, Ellen Campbell embarks on a new life in Australia, a dangerous voyage into the unknown, to marry James, a man she has never met. Helping to nurse a sick passenger, Ellen meets and falls in love with Richard Gray, the ship's doctor. Convinced that he does not return her feelings, she dreads reaching Sydney and having to decide whether to honour her promise to James or face life alone in a strange country.